BONASA PRESS

— Copyright © 2003 Charles R. Meck —
All rights reserved, including the right to reproduce this book or portions thereof in any form.

For information about this book, contact
BONASA PRESS
1502 Water Street • Columbia, PA 17512
Telephone & Fax: (717) 684-4215
www.bonasapress.com

Printed in the United States of America
by Jostens, Inc.
State College, Pennsylvania

BOOK AND DUST JACKET DESIGN
John D. Taylor

ILLUSTRATIONS
Robert Clement Kray

PHOTOGRAPHY
Charles R. Meck

ISBN 0-9725594-2-6

Books By Charles R. Meck

101 Innovative Fly Tying Tips

*The Hatches Made Simple:
A Universal Guide to Selecting
The Right Fly at the Proper Time*

Patterns, Hatches, Tactics and Trout

How to Catch More Trout

*Trout Streams and Hatches of Pennsylvania:
A Complete Flyfishing Guide
To the State's Rivers And Their Hatches* (3rd Ed.)

*Arizona Trout Streams and Their Hatches:
Flyfishing the High Deserts of
Arizona and Western New Mexico*

Great Rivers—Great Hatches

Fishing Small Streams with a Fly Rod

*Mid-Atlantic Trout Streams and Their Hatches:
Overlooked Angling in Pennsylvania,
New York and New Jersey*

Meeting and Fishing the Hatches

*So You Think You're a Fisherman:
What Every Fisherman Should Know*

Memory Rising

Hatches, Waters & Trout

by
Charles R. Meck

Illustrated by
Robert Clement Kray

Contents

Acknowledgements
vi

Introduction
ix

CHAPTER 1
That'll Catch Trout..PAGE 11

CHAPTER 2
Five Bucks And Change...PAGE 21

CHAPTER 3
Tell'Em Who You Are, Vince...................................PAGE 33

CHAPTER 4
I'm Really Proud Of You..PAGE 43

CHAPTER 5
The Hatch Of The Year..PAGE 53

CHAPTER 6
Alone On The Bitterroot River.................................PAGE 63

CHAPTER 7
Blackflies, Gray Skies And Green Drakes................PAGE 73

CHAPTER 8
Horses, Pain And Pleading......................................PAGE 83

CHAPTER 9
A Winter Of Tricos..PAGE 93

CHAPTER 10
Ten For Ten...Well, Almost..PAGE 103

• ORIGINAL ART & PHOTOGRAPHS.......SPECIAL INSERT •

CHAPTER 11
The Intruder..PAGE 113

CHAPTER 12
The Upside Down Drakes..PAGE 123

CHAPTER 13
You'll Never Make It..PAGE 133

CHAPTER 14
A Once-In-A-Lifetime Hatch......................................PAGE 143

CHAPTER 15
I Still Get Excited..PAGE 153

CHAPTER 16
They're Trying To Kill Me..PAGE 165

CHAPTER 17
Great Rivers, Great Hatches,
Great Guides And Great Memories............................PAGE 179

CHAPTER 18
Sink That Fly..PAGE 189

CHAPTER 19
Okay, Now Catch A Trout..PAGE 199

CHAPTER 20
The Case For Catch And Release..................................PAGE 209

CHAPTER 21
My Secret Stream..PAGE 221

CHAPTER 22
The Plastic Man..PAGE 231

CHAPTER 23
The Power Of The Press...PAGE 241

BIBLIOGRAPHY..PAGE 247

INDEX..PAGE 249

Acknowledgements

How do I thank all of the people who have helped me over the years? How do I thank those who have put up with some of my pranks and my naivete? Believe me, plenty of anglers have had to. Many of these important people who have done much for me have already passed into the wide beyond where they catch a lunker trout with every cast—Russ Mowry; Tom Taylor; Lloyd Williams; my dad, Ted Meck; my younger brother, Harold. All helped me in my fly fishing experience in many important ways. Other angling friends have encouraged my writing—Craig Josephson; Paul Weamer; Bob Budd; Bruce Matolyak; Steve McDonald; Frank Nofer; Gary Hitterman; Virgil Bradford; my son, Bryan; my brother, Jerry Meck; and my wife, Shirley. They have fished with me or have encouraged me. I owe a debt of gratitude to them all.

"STUDYING INSECTS IN CONNECTION WITH TROUT FISHING is like living in a house with a million rooms. Opening a door to any of these only reveals the contents of that room—and some more doors. But as long as one is not overcome by the enormity of the task and proceeds one room at a time, a lifetime of joyous learning lies ahead."

CHARLES E. BROOKS
Nymphing for Larger Trout

Introduction

TALK ABOUT GETTING DOWN TO SOMEONE'S LEVEL when you give a talk: Recently, I gave several talks to first graders about writing books and fly fishing. I showed them all the books I had written and I asked what the books had in common. Several youngsters eagerly raised their hands to blurt out that many of the books had the word "hatches" in their title. "Tell me what a hatch is?" I asked. Immediately, they said that it was a chick breaking out of an egg, which makes sense from a child's point of view.

What I was really talking about, of course, was the insects that appear on the surface of a stream, river or lake, and often create trout feeding frenzies, the water boiling with the rises of fish slurping bugs from the surface. Not only aquatic insects—mayflies, caddis flies and stoneflies—but terrestrials (land borne insects) can also fall onto the water's surface in heavy enough numbers to create a hatch. Anyone who has fished in late August can attest to the importance of the winged ant, for example. During August, this terrestrial often falls onto trout waters by the thousands and trout feed for hours on this bonanza. Caterpillars, ants, beetles, grasshoppers and plenty of other insects can bring trout to the surface.

When talking about hatches, I always liken a hatch and trout feeding on the insects to the artificial situation created in a trout hatchery. When fed pellets, trout often lose their timidity and feed voraciously. Add a good number of insects to a stream and the trout there do the same thing—they devour as many insects as they can while the hatch continues. On some streams, hatches don't come along very often, so trout overeat to compensate for numerous barren days. The heavier and longer the hatch, the better your chances of catching trout. Yet hatches can be too heavy. I've seen Green Drakes, Brown Drakes,

Hendricksons and many others on the water in numbers that dwarf the importance of your individual pattern. At times I've quit because I failed to compete for the trout's attention with an imitation.

I have fished the hatches—actively hunting for them—for more than 35 years. The hatches and the waters that brought them to life have created many long-lasting, pleasant memories, ones that have stayed with me for decades, some for almost half a century.

I've shared many hatches with other anglers: I'll never forget that early April day when several friends and I guided Dick Cheney and two of his aides on a small public stream. Or the time the fly fishing video director and producer called for me to catch a trout—immediately. Or the late season White Fly hatches that bring crowded angling—it often looks like opening day—well into the summer.

Experiencing some hatches, I've been alone, such as the fantastic hatch of Green Drakes that appeared on the surface upside down nearly 30 years ago. Or the first time I used a sunken Trico to imitate egg-laying spinners, a pattern that changed my way of fishing spinner falls forever. Then there's the Green Drakes of the North and the giant brook trout that fed on them, too.

Certain hatches stand out more than others. Most I retain because they bring pleasant memories of a great hatch, a great fly to match the hatch, fishing friends and plenty of trout. Some hatches will linger always, like fishing the hatch on a small southeastern Pennsylvania stream shortly after I graduated from high school. These recollections will remain with me even during "senior moments," which I won't admit to having, just yet. Maybe—if I'm lucky—my "senior moments" will be spent in recalling matching these treasured hatches.

All of these elements—the hatches, the streams, the people and much more—are blended into this lifetime of fly fishing recollections.

Charles R. Meck
Autumn, 2003

Chapter 1
That'll Catch Trout

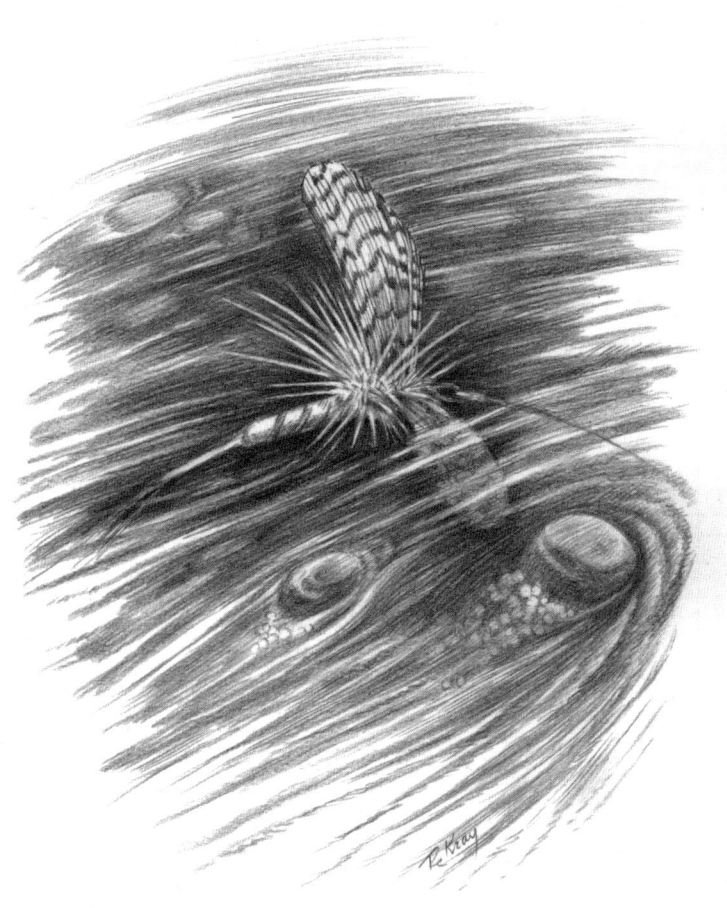

"WE WISH TO REPRODUCE as nearly as possible the effect of the insect as it floats upon the stream; to deceive trout that have had enough experience of flies and of fishermen makes them a bit shy and crafty."

THEODORE GORDON
from *The Quotable Fisherman*
Nick Lyons

———•———

"WHEN YOU ARE COMPLAINING about the selectivity of trout, bear the thought in mind: were it not for this fortunate trait, how long would our stream fishing last?"

ART FLICK
Streamside Guide

That'll Catch Trout

It was 1967, and I had begun to be quite involved in fly fishing and fly tying. That year Penn State transferred me to the Wilkes-Barre Campus, a new job as a Director of Continuing Education, where one of my first official duties was to plan the spring series of informal courses, deemed "informal" because no grades are assigned for course classes.

As part of the evening program, I offered a 15-week, late-January fly tying course for $20—a bargain for 30 hours of instruction, especially considering that the fly tying materials were free. But, I wondered, would anyone register? In the late 1960s fly fishing hadn't yet reached the realm of majesty it has since the 1990's. Not too many anglers tied their own flies. Yet the Wyoming Valley was a hotbed of fly fishing and fly tying—had been for years, because it was home for Stan Cooper, one of the finest tiers in the nation. Stan taught fly tying to many anglers, and his son, Stan, Jr., tied commercially thousands of flies in dozens of patterns.

My concerns were answered when we registered 20 people for that first class. We ended up offering the same fly tying program four years in a row, and just about the same people registered each January. It was a happening in the area, an event many wanted to attend.

John Hagen, Jack Conyngham, Guthrie Conyngham, Charlie Epstein, Rollie Snowden and many other Wyoming Valley residents attended those courses. Most of them were wealthy enough to have somebody tie flies for them, but they enjoyed the class, the camaraderie and the genuine education that took place. We learned a lot from each other.

Our instructor was the late John Perhach. For years, John tied flies for Orvis. His Quill Gordon, Red Quill and Hendrickson dries were truly works of art. John could easily tie 10 dozen flies in an evening—and each was perfect. Annually he'd tie hundreds of dozens of flies. He learned fly tying under the excellent tutelage of Stan Cooper, Sr. (Stan was such an important fly tying and fly fishing figure in northeastern Pennsylvania that the region's Trout Unlimited chapter was named in his honor.)

John probably taught me more about fly tying than other person. I learned many fly tying skills from him: He taught me how to place the wings on a dry fly correctly, how to wind hackle for a dry fly, how to tie on two hackles at the same time and more.

In class, John would normally tie a fly to demonstrate a new pattern. The students went up front to watch him tie, then went back to their desks to try to duplicate the pattern. John tied popular patterns, Quill Gordon and Light Cahill dry flies, and March Brown, Muddler and Wooly Bugger wet flies and streamers.

After a year or two of tying, the wet flies tied by the class looked great. Some of the dry flies were another story, however. Dick Mills (the campus' Bookstore Manager) and I watched and critiqued individual tiers as they tied their copies of the fly John had demonstrated.

After each student tied a pattern Dick, John and I would evaluate it. The three of us agreed never to say that the pattern was no good. Rather, we'd say, "that'll catch trout," if we thought the pattern was a bit less than satisfactory. Often these less-than-adequate patterns had one wing shorter than the other, a wing missing on a dry fly, wings shorter or longer than they should be, too heavy or too long a tail, legs too short. The class members often tied dry flies that had too few hackle fibers, causing the fly to sink rather than float. "That'll catch trout" became a rallying cry and immediately told the tier that the pattern was a bit less than standard.

Still, many student tiers really improved over the years. However, two tiers in particular didn't progress at all. Even in their fourth year, those two tiers remained beginners.

One evening, while all the students were up at the front desk watching John tie a new pattern, Dick Mills and I took a Royal Coachman demonstration dry that John had just tied and placed it in the vise of one of one of the students whose tying skills hadn't improved much. After John had completed tying the new pattern, the students went back to their desks to tie the new pattern. When the student with the fly we placed in his vise came back to his desk, he just stared at the fly for several seconds, then looked up at Dick and me, and, in all seriousness said, "I think I am really getting better." Dick and I exchanged glances, but didn't have the heart to tell him we'd planted that fly in his vise. We never told another soul—until now.

The "final exam" we gave was interesting, too: We bought trout, planted them in a small pond that Frank Michaels owned, and on the final night had the class members fish for them. Can you imagine submitting a bill for $150 to Penn State University for the purchase of 50 trout? No one ever questioned the bill. The students had to use a fly that they tied in the course to catch a trout to finish earning their certificate of completion. As the students caught a trout, I'd rush over to them and formally present them with their certificate.

We planned to end the fishing session at 8 p.m., but a couple students didn't catch any trout during one graduation evening, and refused to quit. They fished until well after dark, desperately trying to hook a fish, yet weren't successful. (We still gave them their certificate, mostly on the basis of persistence), fish or not.

That fly tying course at the Wilkes-Barre campus was 40 years ago. It gained popularity because it provided a reason and a gathering place for fly fishers. Each Wednesday in January, February, March and April the faithful would get together, tie flies and talk fishing tactics, with actual productive tying an added bonus. Our rallying cry, "that'll catch trout" even made its way into several graduation ceremonies. As we handed out the certificates, we'd tell the student "that'll catch trout."

After one graduation, the entire group came to my basement for a reception and celebration of the upcoming fishing season. I served drinks and food and we sat and chatted until midnight.

On another occasion, to celebrate the opening of the trout season in a couple days, I asked the owner of a local trout hatchery to stop by. He brought a tub of trout ranging from 10 to15 inches long, so while we chatted that evening we had trout swimming in a tub in front of us. This was a graduation party I'll never forget, because four days after the party, my wife scented a strange odor rising from the basement. The odor grew stronger and more putrid every day. She eventually found the cause: A slightly inebriated party guest had placed one of the large trout behind one of our steam pipes!

In 1972 I moved from the Wilkes-Barre Campus to the main campus at University Park, which ended the fly tying course for me. I found Spring Creek near the university and it quickly became one of my top local trout waters.

Late one afternoon, along a stretch of Spring Creek's productive limestone waters just below Bellefonte, Don Baylor (a Stroudsburg, Pennsylvania high school teacher, as well as a skilled entomologist and a truly expert fly fisher) and I got into the midst of a great Sulfur hatch.

We fished over trout rising to those Sulfurs for more than two hours. Thousands of duns emerged, but only a few stayed on the surface. Trout fed only on the mayflies that didn't escape quickly. Curious, I grabbed one of the struggling duns and examined it closely. It remained on the surface because it had only one complete wing. The other wing was mutilated, which made the insect incapable of flying. Another laggard Sulfur had the nymphal shuck still attached to the rear of its body. This resembled the imperfect long, heavy tails some of Wilkes Barre students had tied. A third surface-caught mayfly had incomplete legs.

In a moment of enlightenment, it dawned on me: not one of the mayflies that stayed on the surface—the ones that the trout fed on so eagerly—was perfect. Each had a defect—something that kept the mayfly from escaping the water's grasp.

Suddenly, what I said years before in that fly tying class made a lot of sense. Those patterns that we so kindly described as "that'll catch trout" really would. Trout look for imperfections, and the less-than-perfect flies were good imitations of crippled duns. Why shouldn't trout take these imperfect flies, just as they take imperfect nymphs?

Shortly after that incident, I wrote a *Pennsylvania Angler and Boater* article, "When My Poorest Tied Flies Work Best," that described why imperfect patterns work, why a pattern torn to almost a bare hook catches fish. (I've had this happen often.) I also realized the laugh was on me. Years ago, we kidded students who tied less-than-perfect patterns—impressed with our own abilities, we thought we were savvy trout anglers. In the almost 40 years that have passed since that unforgettable fly tying class and that illuminating moment in a hatch, "that'll catch trout" no longer means a poor pattern to me. It now suggests a fly that might better copy the natural on the surface—especially if it's a cripple—and that'll catch trout.

Chapter 2

Five Bucks And Change

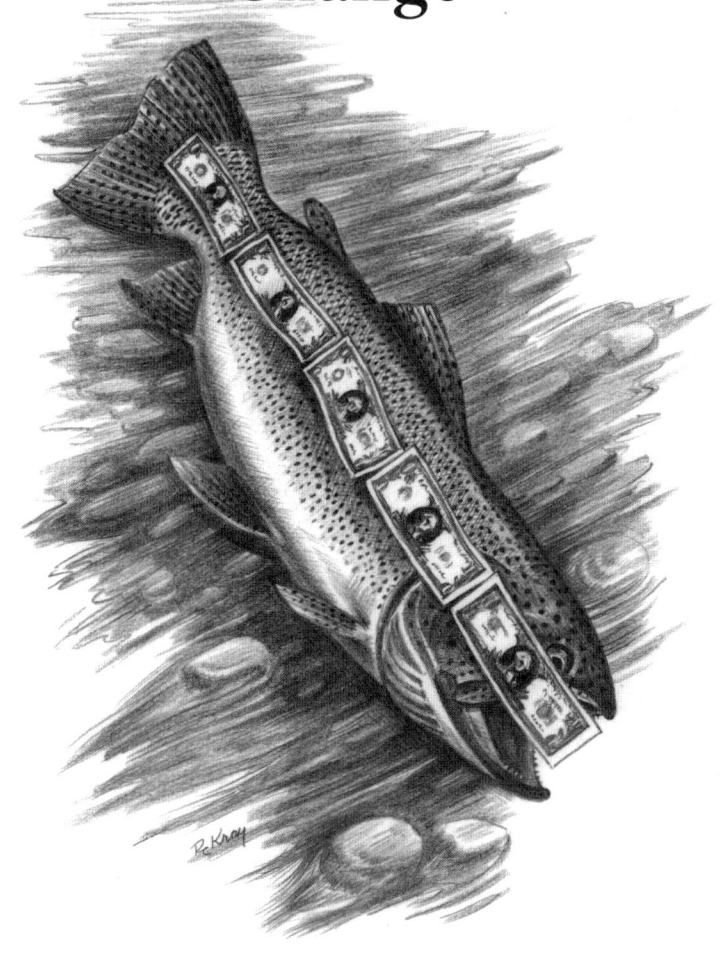

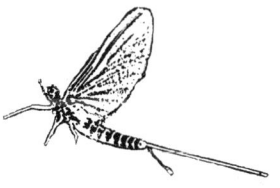

"It is the deepest self, fishing is the most solitary sport, for at its best, it's all between you and the fish."

Arnold Gingerich
American Trout Fishing

———•———

"Fly Fishermen who haven't fished stoneflies, or who have fished them only occasionally, don't realizes what opportunities imitations of these insects offer to anglers."

Eric Leiser and Robert H. Boyle
Stoneflies for the Angler

A heavy trout caught on the Eglinton River in New Zealand.

Five Bucks And Change

New Zealand, a trout angler's dream, and in the middle of the winter, no less .... I sat on the plane before takeoff and mulled those words—and taking an early retirement from Penn State University to do this—over in my mind and smiled.

I had left the State College, Pennsylvania airport at 9 a.m.—arriving just 15 minutes before the flight, thanks to a car that wouldn't start after being left out in minus-20 degree weather all night. (Thank god State College's airport is small and that this was prior to September 11, 2001.)

The flight plan was complicated: Pittsburgh, Chicago, then Portland, Oregon. At Portland I picked up my fishing friend, Mike Manfredo who had orchestrated the trip. From Portland, we went to Los Angeles, Honolulu, then New Zealand—first stop Auckland, then Christchurch.

Talk about jet lag! The flight took more than 25 hours, most spent unhappily awake. We managed a few catnaps, but felt tired and beaten disembarking in Christchurch. Most of the passengers aboard the Honolulu to Auckland flight were bound for Sydney, Australia and the Americas' cup—but Mike and I were going fishing.

To make things even better, with seven airports and plane changes, no luggage joined us when we arrived in balmy New Zealand. Air New Zealand had no idea where our luggage went astray, but they asked for our itinerary so they could transport our belongings to us, once they were found.

Wow! Things were off to a good start. To have paid $1,200 for a trip to one of the world's top trout fishing areas, and have no fishing equipment, no clothes, nothing!

We spent two frustrating days waiting for our fishing gear to arrive at a motel near Omarama. I was tired from the lengthy flight and angry for not being able to fish for two days. Twelve thousand miles from home—in a fly fisher's paradise—without my fishing gear....All we could do was talk about the rivers we wanted to fly fish and sample Kiwi food and beverages: The food was edible but very bland. The restaurant only had iced coffee and hot tea. (I prefer those two drinks the other way around.) I remember calling my wife that first evening and when she asked how the food was, I asked her if she ever heard of a New Zealand restaurant in the United States.

On the runway, the rancher and pilot who was taking us into the bush cautioned us that if the winds picked up—a daily occurrence in those climes—we'd be forced to spend the night in the sheepherder's cabin (his bony finger pointed to a distant shack up a steep mountainside) until the winds calmed and he could land.

I'd be lying if I said I was comfortable about this arrangement. We were in the middle of nowhere, 50 miles from the nearest home, and the probability of an overnight stay in the totally isolated valley was high, if New Zealand winds were true to form. To make matters worse, my blood pressure medicine (I was already two days behind) was in my lost luggage. And what about dinner!

"Stay up there until tomorrow morning," the pilot said in his New Zealand dialect. "If the winds subside I'll be here. But if they don't it might be a day or two before I come back for you."

Now this was our third day of a month in New Zealand, and I understood only a few of the pilot's words. (It took about two weeks to translate their intriguing dialect.) The words I understood scared me: a "day or two" meant we'd have to live off the snacks we carried with us as food. Besides, it would take us a couple hours to hike up that mountain to reach the sheepherder's cabin.

A huge population of Dingle Burn sand flies bit us all day that day. Those winds created a third problem, one not related to our return flight. I knew the same mid-afternoon winds that could keep us grounded could make even a skilled caster frustrated. Earlier that week, I quit fishing several times because the gusts made it impossible. On top of this, I had decided to lug a heavy camcorder with me on every leg of that trip. My intention was a video, something that never happened, yet the camcorder didn't go away; it remained a 10-pound, 20-inch burden in that secluded valley. Even with all the problems and potential problems, though, we were happy; the trout were there.

New Zealand's trout waters are world-famous. This is Lumsden, The Wishing Well, where we ate breakfast every morning.

The fishing was good. I was glad I had the camcorder when Jeff started catching a number of big rainbows, some 28 inches long, that day. I caught a few smaller fish. We fished our way up the isolated and spectacular Dingle Burn valley to another weed patch the rancher called a landing spot.

About 6:30 p.m., I heard a slight noise. The plane? The noise grew louder and louder and finally Jeff and I saw the Piper Cub circle the valley three or four times before it got low enough to land.

Mike Manfredo finally caught up with us the next day—and so did our luggage. For the next two weeks we were headed south. We passed Mt. Cook and the aptly-named Remarkables—the huge geologic wonders of mountains that jut into Lake Wakatipu—near Queenstown.

We set up our headquarters about 70 kilometers south of Queenstown in the Lumsden, Gore, Lake Te Anau area. For the next three weeks we fished some of the most productive rivers on the southern end of the South Island.

Our final destination for the month-long trip was the spectacular waters of the Lake Te Anau area, including the Worsley and Eglinton Rivers.

The boat trip across Lake Te Anau was fantastic. Lake Te Anau is only 30 miles from Milford Sound on South Island's western coast.

The area is drenched in 200 inches of annual rainfall, the source of both the cascading streams and the large, fast-flowing rivers that fill the lake. Motoring across the lake—it was clear 20 feet down—we traveled through a miniature rain forest. The far shore's vegetation reminded me of prehistoric plants, and ferns still wet from rain dotted the mountains.

At the mouth of the Worsley River we saw a 60-foot waterfall, the only kiwi (bird) of the trip, and hundreds of trout over two feet long cruising the 10-foot-deep water. These behemoth rainbows scattered as the boat moved over them.

We anchored the boat at the mouth of the Worsley and, with difficulty, hiked upstream. The edge of the riverbed was filled with huge rounded rocks that made even the best hikers cautious walking over them. Our guides spent the day searching the river for trout. When they spotted a good trout, they called us to fish over the lunker. I landed one fish the entire day. It was 23 inches long. Mike caught at least three fat stream-bred rainbows.

Up to this point, we'd seen only three sporadic hatches in 25 days of fishing. We saw mayflies emerge on the Waikaia River just east of Lumsden one afternoon. Local anglers called the artificial that matched the hatch Dad's Favourite. We matched the hatch with a Size 16 dark brown dry fly and caught trout, but the fish were exceptionally spooky. We had to crawl 50 feet to the edge of the river, and then cast to a rise or the trout would scatter. I'm convinced the extremely clear water made the trout spooky.

On another day, near Lundsen on Mataura River, we hit a great hatch of little Blue-Winged Olives. That notable river holds hatches many days of the season.

One morning crossing the Oreti River on our way to breakfast, I saw a dozen trout feeding on the surface, and asked Mike to stop the car. When the trout appeared, breakfast was an afterthought. The rise rings of a dozen trout upriver revealed their feeding stations. Car parked, we grabbed our gear and were fishing within minutes. What appeared to be spent Quill Gordon spinners were on the surface. Both of us tied on Quill Gordon imitations and began casting. The spinner fall lasted an hour, and we caught half a dozen trout—all over 20 inches long.

On the very last day of the New Zealand adventure, Mike and I fished the Eglinton River, along Route 64. Mike wanted to fish one section, I another, so we parted, going in opposite directions for the morning. We agreed to meet back at the car at noon and compare notes.

At river's edge, I noticed some huge rise forms, including a small pool and riffle section where three fat fish were working. This was unusual, because we hadn't experienced active hatches very often.

Scanning the surface to see what brought the trout up, I saw a trio of down-wings flutter past me. I captured one, examining the black-bodied stonefly closely. A Size 12 Black Stonefly imitation—it reminded of the Early Brown stonefly found near my Pennsylvania home—would probably fill the bill. Both the New Zealand down wing and the Early Brown Stonefly tend to appear on the water's surface. In the United States, the nymphs crawl to a stick, rock or bridge abutment to emerge out of the water. Trout get rare opportunities to capture them. But on South Island this stonefly emerged in the river. Trout had ample opportunity to feed on them. Still, I didn't know how much time I had, how long trout would feed on the stoneflies.

I tied a Size 12 on my leader, and laid a cast over the first trout, the 4X tippet rolling out perfectly.

The trout moved a foot to take the imitation, and the fight was on. The fish shook its head to lose the fly, but couldn't. I landed the 20-plus-inch rainbow after a short run upriver.

Wanting to make the most of the moment—I had no idea how long this hatch would last—I hurried three casts to the next trout. It took the same down-winged pattern and fought up through the riffle to the next small pool. I finally netted this thick rainbow, a bit over 20 inches, a hundred feet above where I started, then returned downriver.

A third trout rose at the head of the pool where it met the fast riffle. In the clear, rich current, I could see the trout holding in the slack of a boulder-created riffle. It looked like a substantial fish.

Lucky for me I took my blood pressure medicine that morning. Face to face with what might be the largest fish of the entire month, I was nervous, excited beyond control, and my casting showed it.

The first cast over the riser went too far to the right and drifted aimlessly before I ended the drift. The second cast wasn't much better, landing three feet to the left of the hungry trout. I also stopped that drift short. On the third cast, the down-wing pattern fell short—two feet below the fish.

Practice makes perfect...on the fourth cast—the one I'll always remember—the fly landed gently two feet above and directly in line

*This is the fish—
five bucks and
change.*

with the feeding trout. Perfect....

When the fly floated over the trout, I saw a huge, dark thing—it almost looked like a long black log—swim up, take the fly, then sink back down towards the bottom.

When I set the hook, the big rainbow dove, then ran up through the riffle into the next pool, shaking its head to cast the fly from its mouth.

The fish was huge, unlike anything I had encountered in 40 years of fishing. We battled for about fifteen minutes before I brought it to the net. One gigantic problem: That monster trout wouldn't fit in the net. Forgetting about catch and release for a moment, I scooped the monster on to the sand.

Could this be the fish I came to New Zealand for, my 30-inch trophy? I wanted to measure that huge rainbow. Just how long was it? I had no ruler, no measure on my rod, none on my net. All I had was the dollar bills in my wallet—something I had used before, because a dollar is (conveniently enough) just a fraction longer than six inches. With the fish wriggling for the freedom of the river, I laid the dollar bill at the tip of its snout...one, two, three, four, five. The rainbow measured a bit over five dollar bills, more than 30 inches long—the fish I had come to New Zealand to experience.

I wanted Mike to see this trout, but Mike could be a couple miles downriver, and my voice wouldn't carry above the thundering roar of the fast-flowing Eglinton. If I told him, he would never believe the size of the rainbow, so I did the best I could, shot half a dozen hurried photos of my trophy in a curled up position—otherwise he wouldn't fit in the camera's frame—then gently slipped the trout back into the icy river.

I was back at the car early. I knew I couldn't top that catch. About an hour later Mike came back. He talked about the hatch and catching some nice trout, then asked how I had done. I told him, and when the size question came up, I proudly said "five bucks and change."

What a way to end a glorious month in one of the friendliest fishing spots on the globe. We saw kiwis and breathtaking mountains, heard thunderous waterfalls, and caught huge rainbows and browns. Yet the island's friendly people made it all come together. There's more to fly fishing than just casting and catching trout. This is just a small part of the process—camaraderie, sharing stories, meeting new friends, these are the important things in fishing. To show how much this means, when Mike and I left Waikaia, more than half the people in town came out to wish us well on the rest of our trip.

If you ever get a chance to visit New Zealand, make certain you mingle with these friendly people.

CHAPTER 3

Tell 'Em Who You Are, Vince...

"The next serious problem arises from the sheer abundance of insects on the water. Your artificial is competing with so many of the naturals that getting the attention of the trout seems hopeless."

———•———

"On all spiner patterns, keep the hackle thin. If the hackle turns out so thick that it obscures the body, cut away some fibers at the top and bottom. No matter what pattern you use, do not lose confidence in it if it is not immediately taken. *Caenis* fishing requires a lot of precision casting, and even then your fly is just one item among the many naturals that will be floating by the trout. So don't give up. The important thing is to get the trout to see your fly."

———•———

"Thus, we must arrive at one of the really great differences between limestone and freestone rivers and that is the matter of stability."

Vincent C. Marinaro
In The Ring Of The Rise

This is Falling Springs Branch, near Chambersburg, Pennsylvania, where Vince Marinaro tried to catch trout during a Trico spinner fall.

Tell'em Who You Are, Vince...

VINCE MARINARO WAS A TREMENDOUS WRITER, an innovator of productive fly patterns and a consummate investigator. His *Ring of the Rise* and *A Modern Dry Fly Code* were innovations, classics in fly fishing literature. His thorax dry fly was a true work of art. Marinaro suggested timeless patterns that work as well today as they did when he wrote about them. His study of trout feeding behavior, particularly classifying trout rise forms, and how each rise indicates the manner in which a fish is feeding, was truly innovative.

I first met Vince Marinaro in the summer of 1969, fishing the Trico hatches he loved to chase on Falling Springs, a limestone stream, near Chambersburg, Pennsylvania. We met through Barry Beck, now a familiar fishing name, then an up-and-coming angler. Barry's fishing prowess impressed me from the very first time I met and fished with him. Barry caught trout when nobody else did. Barry's wife, Cathy, has also become a world-renowned angler.

Vince chased Trico hatches across Pennsylvania with a passion. On Pennsylvania's streams, the diminutive Trico usually begins hatching in late June and continues well into October and sometimes November. During the heat and humidity of summer, the hatch and the spinner fall can begin and end in less than an hour. The tiny mayflies must complete their life cycle quickly. As autumn approaches and the days cool, however, the hatch and spinner fall can sometimes be fished near noon—even later.

In addition to being a Trico chaser, Vince was also an astute attorney, and, occasionally, a curmudgeon. He could get grumpy and moody when things didn't go his way, something George Harvey can tell you about, some wild fishing stories when Vince, George and others fished together. Still, most anglers (me, too), will remember Vince as one of fly fishing's innovators.

For years Vince and other notables like Charlie Fox fished the famous Trico hatches on southcentral Pennsylvania's limestone streams—Falling Springs, Yellow Breeches and the LeTort Spring Run. All of these waters held great late summer Trico spinner falls and a good supply of trout.

One late July day, about 30 years ago, Barry Beck, Dick Mills, Vince and I were fishing the Trico hatch on Falling Springs. Even then I considered Barry Beck one of the finest fly fishers I had ever seen. I had fished quite often with Barry, and recognized him immediately as a highly skilled fishing machine. I didn't know it then, but within a few years he would become one of the better-known fly fishers in the world.

At that time, Falling Springs had one of the heaviest concentrations of Trico mayflies of any stream in the East, though I'm sad to say that today, Falling Springs has lost much of its Trico population (thanks to suburbanization and its accompanying runoff problems).

We arrived early that morning, the sun peeking over a steep hill to the east, and saw numerous duns still emerging. The four of us sat back and chatted for almost half an hour before a pod of trout rose to the first spent female spinners floating past them.

The initial plan was for me to go first on our beat of the stream. Me fish in front of Barry Beck and Vince Marinaro? No way! I was intimidated by the idea of Vince watching me fish over Trico-rising trout. I was terrified he'd criticize my casting, my presentation. So I passed on the offer, content to sit back, learn from the master.

As he often did with this hatch, Vince jumped into action. More than a dozen trout rose to the tiny white and brown spinners drifting spent-winged on the surface. Vince cast to the nearest consistent riser, just 20 feet upstream. One cast, two, three, four—none were productive. All refused Vince's imitation. (In fairness, these trout had been fished over many times during this Trico season.) We could all detect some frustration in Vince's action and his tone of voice. You could hear a low growl emanating from Vince's stream of consciousness. He was getting increasingly annoyed—and less confident. He wasn't a happy soldier. He tried other rising trout, mumbling almost inaudibly. Five casts, six, seven, eight—but not one strike. Not one of those frequent risers even looked at Vince's spent-wing fly.

Dick, Barry and I detected a slight decibel rise in the mumbling, more frustration in Vince's efforts. Finally, Barry, none too shy about commenting on Vince's dissatisfactions, blurted out, "Tell the trout who you are, Vince. Tell them you wrote the book about Tricos."

Vince mumbled something unintelligible directed at Barry and continued to fish.

I fished very little that morning, figuring that if Vince Marino, the dean of the Trico anglers couldn't catch trout, I wouldn't stand a chance.

The Trico hatches on those Pennsylvania waters were alike: With heavy angling pressure and a hatch and spinner fall that continues uninterrupted for more than three months, the trout became highly selective, to the point of fly fisher annoyance. The fish inspected everything—the leader, the fly, how it rides the water, angles, colors, even your knots—refusing almost anything with a hook. I've had days where trout drift with perfect imitations, inspecting them carefully, then turning away.

We left Falling Springs that day with new respect for the hatch, the spinner fall and for those disgustingly selective trout. This heavy pressure often continues well into October and on almost every day you'll find the same fly fishers fishing the same spinner fall.

Later, I found that the best time to fish the Trico hatch is when it begins, late June or early July, when trout haven't seen too many patterns or too much pressure.

Two years after the four of us fished the Trico on Falling Springs, Vince visited Barry's home in north central Pennsylvania for some August freestone fly fishing. Pennsylvania's freestone waters usually don't have the limestone buffer that streams like Falling Springs do, hence fewer hatches. These same freestone streams usually run lower and warmer in midsummer compared to the limestone streams. I've seen good Trico hatches on many freestone streams with temperatures too high for any trout population.

I visited with Vince during his first evening at Barry's. Had he ever fished a freestone Trico hatch? Vince's eyes lit up. He hadn't, but wanted to see one. Barry had made plans for their morning's fly fishing, but Vince convinced him that those plans could wait because he wanted to see a freestone Trico hatch.

The lower end of Bowman Creek, just 30 miles east of Barry, had terrific Trico hatches that few anglers fished in the late season. Sharing this, I sensed Vince's keenness immediately, the excitement in his voice. Yet I felt apprehension. I had changed Vince's schedule—I'd better be right. This time, both Vince and Barry were depending on me. We decided to rendezvous at Bowman's special regulations (Fly Fishing Only) area at dawn.

That morning, we hurried to rig our gear and headed upstream. We were lucky in at least one sense—no other anglers. As guide, I hoped the hatch would appear, the spinners would fall and trout would rise to them—a lot of variables.

Half a mile upstream, walking through heavy early morning dew, we found a section with a relatively open canopy. (Trico mating rituals require an open area. Heavy cover over the stream prevents this. If you want to see a good spinner fall, look for openings in the canopy, meadows or open fields.) More luck—as we maneuvered to get into a casting position, glistening tiny Trico spinners already formed their mating flight 20 feet above a fast open stretch of water. The first light of dawn breaking through the trees illuminated thousands of tiny mayfly wings. They looked like morning stars hovering above the stream.

Vince was ecstatic, a first for this hardy veteran. He couldn't hide his emotions, and I truly believe he had not encountered a freestone Trico hatch before. Now if the trout would cooperate....

I had just checked the water temperature—64 degrees—everything seemed perfect, and in his own peerless way, Vince was excited.

The section of Bowman Creek where Vince Marinaro caught trout on a Trico.

To my extreme delight, five trout were already feeding on glistening spinners floating down the shallow, late summer water. Vince quickly cast his Size 24 spent-wing just above one of the trout. When the tiny imitation floated over it, the riser immediately sucked it from the surface. Vince landed the nine-inch stocked brown and cast to a second fish. That one, also a small stocked trout, took his pattern on the first drift. Wow, it was all coming together! The spinner fall lasted a bit longer than half an hour. Vince landed his fourth fish when the cluster of spinners above us began to thin, and the rings of rising trout ceased to break the creek's calm surface. In those final few minutes Vince changed to a dark brown male Trico spinner pattern and landed one more trout.

Since 1968, I've kept a fishing diary, a record of every experience—when, where, who accompanied me, the patterns used, the hatches, trout caught, as well as some appropriate remarks. That morning's remarks says, "Vince Marinaro finally saw his first freestone Trico spinner fall and caught five trout." As we walked back to our cars I breathed a giant sigh of relief: We had just fished on a public stream, saw a prolific Trico spinner fall and caught trout matching that spinner. Vince didn't have to tell the trout who he was that day. They—and we—all knew that on that morning, he was Vince Marinaro, stalker of Tricos and trout.

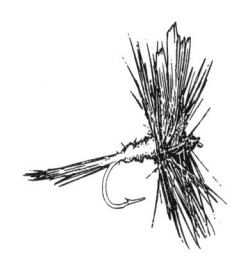

Chapter 4

I'm Really Proud Of You

"As he talked, I was thinking. About trout."
Harry Middleton
The Earth Is Enough

I'm Really Proud Of You

IN THIS TRUE STORY,
SOME NAMES HAVE BEEN CHANGED
TO PROTECT THE INNOCENT....

I FIRST MET RAY THOMAS ON BOWMAN CREEK, just outside Tunkhannock, Pennsylvania—near Wilkes Barre-Scranton—late one May evening in 1969. The two of us acted like kids when we saw Coffin Flies, Green Drake spinners, land on the creek's surface, and trout begin to feed on them. Our large spent-winged patterns caught trout past sunset. Yet before that night neither of us knew the stream held Green Drakes.

Ray was a true conservationist, practicing catch and release fishing long before it was popular. I recall one summer morning Ray and I fished Bowman's Trico spinner fall. His eyesight had begun to fail him and he had trouble with those Size 24 patterns—but he still caught trout that morning.

Ray hated to kill anything. He returned every one of those trout to the stream. He was also concerned about each stream he fished and contributed to the betterment of the environment in many ways, volunteering for stream improvement campaigns on Bowman Creek, working for more hunting land. Ray was an outstanding citizen of the Wyoming Valley.

His one little—you might call it major—idiosyncrasy, however, was road kill: Ray actively looked for and picked up road kill, pavement pizza, the host of pheasants, grouse, squirrels, waterfowl, rabbits, deer and groundhogs that get whacked by cars. Ray picked up a lot of them, took them home and cooked them for dinner. He enjoyed them.

I'm certain it wasn't quite as bad as some people made it out to be, but you know how stories and legends grow. Like the one about the goose that Ray made dinner from—it got whacked thinking wet highway was pond.

One evening we fished Bowman Creek until well after dark. While following him home, I saw Ray's car suddenly pull over to the side of the road. Thinking he was having trouble, I pulled in behind him. While I watched, Ray liberated some dead critter from the yellow lined road. Maybe he saw it on the way to the stream. Don't ask me what it was—too dark—something at least marginally edible.

This happened when I was at the Wilkes-Barre Campus of the Pennsylvania State University. Ray first suggested the campus's the fly tying course, one of the most popular informal offerings in the evening program. Although several years later a promotion took me to University Park in State College, I had an opportunity to visit Wilkes-Barre on a regular basis and I continued to keep in touch with and fish with Ray until he passed away.

Shortly after I arrived in State College, nearly 20 active sportsmen, including angling and hunting friends like Mark Davis, Ned Minshall and Don Fornwalt, began serving a March wild game dinner, often at my home. A way to clean out freezers and to talk about the upcoming fishing season, we had deer, rabbit, pheasant, grouse, and one or two guests might bring trout. Every once in a while someone even brought an exotic game piece like moose, elk or caribou. The meals were fairly good.

After the dinner we would hand out gag awards: best angler, best hunter, the largest game killed, the largest trout released and the best conservationist. We called the conservation award "The Ray Thomas Award for Conservation," and the "trophy" was silly—a piece of cardboard cut to look like a tire-flattened opossum. It was all tongue-in-cheek. I received the Ray Thomas Award that inaugural year. Big deal! It had no meaning. It was just a gag.

As I said, Ned Minshall attended those game dinners. Ned was a fly fisher and the editor of the monthly newsletter for Continuing Education at the university. Ned frequently fly fished on his Penns Creek property. No one thought anything about it when Ned took a few photos of the "awards ceremony." Well, several days after I received that fictitious award, Ned placed a photo and a caption on the award and me in the official Continuing Education newsletter. The caption under the photo read: "Charlie Meck, Regional Director for Continuing Education recently accepted the Ray Thomas Award for his conservation efforts in the state. Charlie received this prestigious award at a recent dinner." When I opened the continuing education newsletter that Monday I was flabbergasted. I started laughing—I thought it was funny that Ned should include that award in the newsletter as a matter of fact and importance.

That same day that the newsletter came out, I received an early morning call from the secretary of the vice president for continuing education, my "big boss." The vice president wanted to see me in his office that afternoon. When the VP calls a meeting you cancel everything. Dread of all dreads! The only time the big boss wanted to see me alone was when I did something wrong. He had scheduled meetings with me twice before and both times reprimanded me—one time summoning me from the Schuylkill Campus, 150 miles away from the university, to see me that afternoon. What had I done to get chewed out about this time? I began to think about my potential litany of crimes, but the list was reasonably short—except for that road kill award. Had the VP heard about the hoax and the photo in the newsletter? Should I enter the meeting ready to confess everything? I asked Donna Hilligas, his secretary, why he wanted to meet with me, but she didn't know. I skipped lunch—I couldn't eat. I was too concerned, too scared about why I was called into his office.

I came to his office nervous that afternoon, both apprehensive and curious about his agenda for the meeting. I hoped I was prepared for the worst. I was ready to apologize—even to say that I had nothing to do with the photo in the newsletter. I didn't want the travesty to go any further.

As I entered his office the VP was beaming—grinning from ear to ear. This was very unusual—he seldom displayed this type of emotion.

His smile was contagious. Evidently I wasn't going to get criticized or chewed out for something. He looked too happy. In fact he had a very unusual smile. I never saw him look like this before or since.

He proudly held up my photo in the newsletter and pointed to it with satisfaction. "Charlie, we are truly proud of you today for winning this prestigious award. You deserve it," he said with pride. "This photo and a note from me about your award will be placed in your personnel file and remain there forever. Thank you for your true sense of conservation. I will also make certain the president of the university

Bowman Creek where Ray Thomas and I fished frequently.

hears about this. We are all truly proud of your efforts in the field of conservation"

You could have blown me over with a small fan on low speed, and I was so stunned that I was uncertain how I should answer him. Should I tell my boss that the whole thing was a hoax—that I really didn't win any award—that we made up the award just for a game dinner?

I didn't do that. I regret to say I didn't take the high road, the moral way out; I took the easy way out. I waited for almost a minute before I thanked him for his consideration and walked out of his office. If he or the president of the university ever found out the truth about our hoax, I'd be canned, since I covered it up—involvement or no involvement. He wouldn't stand for a joke like that.

I called my wife, Shirley, and told her what had happened and swore her to secrecy. As soon as I hung up the phone, I headed up to Ned Minshall's office.

When I told Ned what had just happened his mouth dropped and he looked worried. He swore me to silence and pleaded with me to keep the award and the sham a secret until the vice president retired. One trouble: The vice president didn't plan to retire for at least 10 more years. We had to keep that secret for a decade.

Shortly after that meeting, the vice president held a statewide meeting for all directors and assistant directors of continuing education from all of the Commonwealth campuses. About 50 employees attended the meeting. At the opening of that meeting he asked me to stand and introduced me as the winner of the Ray Thomas Award for Conservation. Again, he complimented me and said that he wished that everyone in the division "would achieve the excellence in the field of conservation that Charlie Meck did."

Oh boy! Was I embarrassed! What would I say to all my fellow workers? I thanked him and encouraged all the others to strive for excellence. Wow—the lie was getting bigger. That's usually what happens with lies—they get bigger and bigger and bigger. They get uncontrollable. You can't stop them. Thank goodness none of the people in the meeting knew of the sham.

For more than 10 years Ned and I kept that award a secret—only my wife and immediate family knew about that hoax. Charlie Meck—Conservationist of the Year—winner of the prestigious Ray Thomas Award: No way! But it sounded good and it remained in my personnel file until the day I retired from the university. Maybe it's still there.

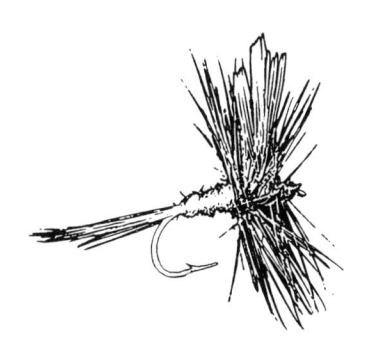

Chapter 5
The Hatch Of The Year

"**O**NE OF THE SEASON'S MOST INTERESTING but under-rate hatches is that of *Paraleptophlebia adoptivia*. This prolific little mayfly is extremely adbundant in the East and Midwest and is usually referred to as the Blue Quill."

AL CAUCCI & BOB NASTASI
Hatches II

The Hatch Of The Year

FRED CILLETTI AND I GO BACK A LONG WAY. Fred was one of my continuing education instructors at Penn State's Pottsville campus. He taught an introductory English course and served as the student government association's advisor. As an elected student government representative, I often talked fly fishing with Fred. When Fred advanced to the university's public relations department at University Park, we never lost touch. So when the university's president asked Fred to find someone to guide his guests, Fred immediately thought of me. That's one reason I was looking forward to Pennsylvania's 1995 trout season with great anticipation. Just before the season began, Fred asked me to take their commencement speaker on a two-day fly fishing trip. Fred said the speaker enjoyed fly fishing and would come to the university early to fish some central Pennsylvania trout streams.

The guest was the man who is now Vice President, Dick Cheney. At that time, the former Secretary of State had retired to a Washington, D.C. think tank. Cheney brought two co-workers: his assistant Andrew Goldman, from New York City, who had never fly fished before; and Shawn O'Keefe, the Secretary of the Navy under the senior Bush administration. O'Keefe, like Cheney, was an accomplished fly angler, as well as a Penn State professor at the time. O'Keefe is a terrific administrator and is presently the head of the National Aeronautics and Space Administration (NASA).

I had retired nine years earlier and had just completed *Pennsylvania Trout Streams and Their Hatches*. Fred Cilletti assured Cheney that if anyone knew where he could catch some central Pennsylvania trout, it would be me.

For the first day of fishing we selected a private section of one of the area's top limestone streams, Spruce Creek—Dave McMullen's Six Springs area. This private water is loaded with huge brown and rainbow trout, many over 20 inches long. Since Andrew had never fly fished before, my son, Bryan Meck, took him downstream a half mile and gave him a quick lesson in fly fishing basics, while the rest of us took up fishing spots. Within 10 minutes Bryan coached Andrew well enough that he landed his first trout, a fat, thick 20-inch Spruce Creek brown trout—not bad for someone who had never held a fly rod in his hands. It wouldn't be Andrew's last trout—he managed to catch a couple more before the day ended. Meanwhile, a few hundred yards upstream, Dick and Shawn caught several large trout over 20 inches long. They would both catch big trout throughout the day.

Dick wanted to see some other water the next day, and asked if we could go to a public stream. I assumed he was tired of big fish and private streams. Bob's Creek, just north of Bedford, a small southwestern Pennsylvania trout stream, seemed like the perfect fit. The chances of seeing a good hatch in mid-April were extremely good because this fertile freestone creek holds the heaviest hatches I've ever encountered of Blue Quills and Quill Gordons, two early season mayflies. In previous years, I had consistently encountered the brace of dark gray mayflies in the afternoon—exactly the time we'd be on the stream. The stream also has an excellent combination of stream-bred and stocked brown trout and a good number of native brook trout.

At its widest, secluded Bob's Creek might be 20 feet across. To reach some of the more productive waters, anglers must walk several miles. I figured that as we hiked upstream away from the road we'd see fewer and fewer anglers.

Two more friends joined us that second day. Coming from many directions, the seven of us agreed to meet the next morning in the parking lot of the Spruce Creek Tavern, located in the town by the same name.

The tavern is known for two—maybe three—things: owner John Carper, its French fries and its barbequed ribs. Some of the local residents in this small town recently erected a sign along one of the highways, a constricted, wandering two-lane, naming it the John Carper Highway in honor of John. Carper is a true character, one of a kind. A tray of the tavern's fries is an adventure. For $2, you get enough fries to bloat an elephant. John's barbecued ribs—made only on special order—are known throughout the state. His ribs are truly memorable. The first night I had ribs at our annual Trout Kickoff dinner, John handed me a huge tray of ribs. I took a couple and passed them on. John quickly handed the tray back to me and told me that was my tray and every other person at the banquet would get the same amount. Good heavens! Really, John just thinks he runs the tavern. His wife Lois and daughter Lori Woodring really run the place and cook the food.

When John saw us in the parking lot he came out to greet us. I asked him if was all right to park Dick's car in his lot while we fished, and John proudly handed Cheney a tavern logo hat and in his own inimitable way said we should hurry up and go fishing. John doesn't give everyone a hat—only dignitaries.

Joining us for the fishing were my son Bryan; my son-in-law

Rick Nowaczek, an FBI agent; and Craig Josephson, a fishing friend. Other friends heard about the trip and asked for a chance to fish with Dick Cheney, but I limited the number of anglers to seven. Where would all those people find a good place to fish on a small public stream the first week of a new trout season?

We met at the tavern at 9 a.m. and were ready to fish Bob's Creek by 10:30 a.m. The third day of the Pennsylvania trout season, I feared heavy crowds would appear on Bob's Creek early. I was correct. By the time we got there, four cars had already emptied their anglers, and for the first half-mile upstream from the parking lot, we hunted for a place to fish. Finally upstream more than a mile from the dirt road, the six of us found plenty of room.

Two things troubled us that day—the heavy angling crowd and a typical drizzly cool mid-April day. The anglers we avoided by hiking upstream. The morning rain turned to a light drizzle, but the air temperature never rose above 50 degrees. I was concerned that no hatch would appear under these conditions. Dick, Bryan and I were approaching a small but deep pool fed by a wide, productive riffle when we saw more than a dozen trout rising. Hundreds of cold-dazed Blue Quills rested on the surface, but very few took flight.

Dick asked what he should use. I turned to Bryan, opened his six-compartment fly box and picked out a Size 18 Blue Quill dry fly. It turned out to be the top fly of the day—of that season. Bryan had two more left and he tied one on Cheney's 5X tippet. "That should work," Bryan said. Then both Bryan and I sat back to watch Dick fish to the baker' dozen trout rising in the pool and riffle above it. Rick and Craig also stopped at the pool to observe. One by one, Dick caught those fish, one after another, up to number 12. Twelve for 13 is superb for matching the hatch on a small, crowded, public stream.

The hatch continued for three hours that afternoon, and after Cheney's 12-trout angling demonstration, all of us headed to separate sections of the stream armed with Size 18 Blue Quills. We all caught trout until 4 p.m., then decided to head back to State College.

Within a mile of the section of Bob's Creek we fished that day, visitors and anglers will find a sign, eulogizing the Lost Children of the Alleghenies, two small girls who got lost in the woods and died. I'd like to erect another sign nearby, something happier, that would read: "In this pool, on April 19, 1995 the future Vice President of the United States, Dick Cheney, caught 12 of 13 trout that rose during a hatch of Blue Quills." And why not? We've affectionately referred to the pool where Dick caught those dozen trout as the Cheney Pool. Dick Cheney demonstrated for us all what can happen when you properly match the Blue Quill hatch.

One of the most important parts of a fishing trip, especially a successful one, is what happens between the anticipation and the fishing—the camaraderie shared over or a meal or drink to discuss and dissect the day's events. Between the hour's ride back to State College, and Dick's invitation for late evening dinner with Shawn, Andrew and him at the State College Hotel (we accepted), we reminisced the day's events, and our success. Later, Bryan, Dick and Rick discussed the tactics in Desert Storm. The bantering went on long after 10 p.m. and would have continued had not Dick's graduation talk preparations interrupted the evening.

Five important aspects made this particular Blue Quill the hatch of the year. 1.) It was by far the heaviest hatch of Blue Quills I had witnessed on any small stream. In each pool and riffle I saw hundreds of resting duns. 2.) More trout rose for this small dark gray mayfly than on the vast majority of other hatches I have seen. I've seen heavier Sulfur, Pale Morning Dun and Green Drake hatches, but never as many trout in a small concentrated area rise to a hatch. 3.) We had the perfect pattern for the hatch. When I held the pattern next to the natural they looked alike, except of course for the hook. 4.) Weather conditions were ideal for an early season Blue Quill hatch. Cold, drizzly weather prevents mayflies from escaping rapidly from the surface. The Blue Quills that afternoon remained on the surface for a long time. 5.) I was the guide—and I had three important guests with me. When guiding, I always fear my guests won't catch trout. I worry about them catching trout before I take them fishing and when they're fishing. I constantly worry that my guests won't have a good time. Boy, did my guests have a good time and did they ever catch trout that day! Without the those emerging mayflies, and their match, a Size 18 Blue Quill, we would have caught trout—but not in the numbers or with the excitement we experienced when we matched the hatch of the day—make it the hatch of the year—on Bob's Creek.

Chapter 6

Alone On The Bitteroot River

"THIS LARGE, JUICY MAYFLY is perhaps the most imporant insect on many Western trout streams. It is on the water for about two weeks and is large enough to coax the really heavy fish to the surface."
                    ERNEST G. SCHWEIBERT, JR.
                         Matching the Hatch

Alone On
The Bitteroot River

I'M TERRIBLY IMPATIENT—gotta get things done immediately. When I have a commitment, I get anxious to the point of obnoxious until I've completed it. I had a deadline to get the manuscript for my first book, *Meeting and Fishing the Hatches*, into Winchester Press by September 1, 1976. It was already the end of June and I still had to write the entire section on western fishing and the hatches found there. I had just completed the Midwestern section with a trip to Michigan and Wisconsin, experiencing great Brown Drake hatches on the Au Sable River in Grayling, Michigan—but the book research wasn't wrapped up yet.

Now I headed West for my introduction to the Rocky Mountains and the fishing there. This was June 1976 and I had never been west of Wisconsin. I had set myself a difficult goal: to fish and write about 20 rivers in six western states and witness at least 10 different hatches. My first leg of that western trip focused on the rivers of Montana and Wyoming. I had contacted two people in Missoula, Montana several weeks before. We talked frequently over the previous month and those two Montana anglers promised to meet with me, tell me about the local hatches, and help me fish their rivers. This was long before many of the western rivers like the Bitteroot had any guides or drift boats, so I had to depend on local anglers for help. Now, of course, the Bitteroot holds many guides.

One local expert agreed to meet me when I got off the plane that late June evening. I waited for an hour in Missoula's small airport but no one showed. I called his home several times. No answer. Then I called a second so-called expert I had talked with. No answer there, either.

I was alone in Montana, 2,000 miles from home, and the two men who had promised to help vanished. I got my rental car and headed to a motel. Maybe tomorrow I could reach one of the two anglers. The return flight to Pennsylvania was three weeks away, so I was stuck until my departure—all dressed up and no place to go. All set to fly fish and no one to take me.

I called my local contacts early the next morning and got no answer. I went to a local diner, ate breakfast and called again. No luck! I finally got the message after trying to reach them a half dozen times. Evidently these local experts did not want to help, despite their promises. They didn't want their local secrets divulged in any book—nice of them to let me know beforehand!

I waited around town that entire day pondering my next move. What would I do? Where would I start? The whole thing almost overwhelmed me. I had a deadline staring me in the face—the contract was signed—so I had to fish some of these rivers, with or without a local expert. I had to make the best of a bad situation.

The next morning, without a guide or any local information, I decided to hit the Bitterroot River just a few miles south of Missoula. Near Victor, I asked a rancher if I could fish on his property. He gave me permission, then I hiked downriver a mile, sat by the river's edge and contemplated my next move. It was late June and the river ran high—maybe a couple feet above its late summer flow, thanks to snowmelt from the mountains in the West.

This was the very first western river I had ever seen. It was high, huge, nothing like those midsummer eastern streams. To me, alone on the Bitterroot River that day meant no hatch, no rising trout, no other anglers, high water and especially no local angler to help me shortcut the local hatch location problem. What would happen next? I felt overwhelmed.

I know God was there, because within an hour spent sitting there feeling sorry for myself, a few huge mayflies appeared right in front of me on those snow-fed waters. Soon dozens of these dark olive gray mayflies—matched with a Size 10 or 12 imitation—fluttered on the surface, and trout in all sections of the river began to feed on them. What for the past hour had been high runoff water void of any rise quickly evolved into a feeding frenzy. The river teemed with huge rising trout, as if somebody tossed trout pellets into a hatchery pond. The fish were wild, chasing every laggard dun that loitered on the roiling surface.

Certain the insect emerging had to be the western Green Drake, I introduced myself to western fishing with a Size 12 Western Green Drake on 4X tippet, and I began casting to one of the 20 rising fish I could see. Seconds later, I had my first Montana trout on the line, a huge rainbow that fought well for five to 10 minutes before I quickly released him. A second rainbow hit the very next cast and I couldn't let go of that trout fast enough. You know the story: The hatch might end as quickly as it began so you want to fish over one more rise before the hatch fades. Yet for two hours I hit the western Green Drake hatch on the Bitterroot—all on my own. After my discouraging start, suddenly this western match-the-hatch business didn't seem too tough.

It ended, of course—no more of those huge dark olive mayflies appeared the surface, no more trout rose, the surface was quiet again—as quickly as it began. The trout disappeared beneath the roiling waters. The surface was again completely still.

The next day I traveled to West Yellowstone just outside Yellowstone National Park. Anyone studying, fishing, or writing about fly fishing in the West's hatches and rivers must include the fishing in and around the park.

I had corresponded with Charlie Brooks, who also promised to help me with the hatches and where to fish, yet I had my doubts about the offer after my Bitterroot experience. Discouraged about my two no-shows, I felt certain he too would back out of his commitment. Charlie was a well-known, well-respected fly fishing writer and I was nobody. He wrote great books like *Fishing Yellowstone Waters*, *Nymph Fishing for Larger Trout* and *The Trout and the Stream*. He created many new patterns, including the Montana Stonefly. And with his *Fishing Yellowstone Waters*, Charlie definitely knew the waters around Yellowstone Park. Why would he want to help me write a book? Besides, when I contacted him, he was ill.

This time, though, I was wrong. Charlie took me under his tutelage and daily told me which stream or river to fish and what hatches I might see. Each evening, after dark, I'd come by Charlie's house and give him a detailed report of my day's activities—the successes (and failures, of which there were many)—and he'd give me suggestions for the next day's fishing. He was the consummate teacher, I the eager pupil.

For two weeks I came to Charlie's house daily and looked to him for further guidance. One day I returned and complained that I was

The Bitterroot River.

tired of fishing warm water. I had fished the Firehole River for two days and saw temperatures into the high 70s, too warm for trout. Charlie sent me off with detailed directions to several extremely cold branches of the Madison River, where I fished over trout in water in the high 50s. One evening we talked about my itinerary for the next day. He sent me to Henry's Fork, just a little over an hour from his house, to see the Brown Drake, western Green Drake and Pale Morning Dun hatches. He gave me an assignment every day to complete. What a fantastic writer and human being! Without his help, *Meeting and Fishing the Hatches* would never have been completed.

One other day July day, after I again complained again about warm waters, Charlie told me to go on the Yellowstone River near Gardiner, Montana, just outside of the park. He said that the Salmon Flies had been emerging the past couple days. I hadn't seen this huge down-wing stonefly, and was eager to experience it in this huge, cold river.

I reached the river a couple hours before dark and saw some giant down-wing insects, big stoneflies, land on the surface. More joined them. Shaking the bushes and trees near shore, I saw thousands of salmon flies. Soon some of the Yellowstone cutthroats began feeding on these monster stoneflies, with trout rising as far as I could see. The Simple Salmon pattern—an orange-bodied stonefly with several sets of elk downwings, tied on a long-shanked hook—tied for me by Nick Nicholas, with Blue Ribbon Anglers—charmed those fish.

Well past 11 p.m., I came back to Charlie's to tell him about the hatch and the fish. I was excited—it couldn't wait until morning. I had to tell him that great matching the hatch episode with the salmon fly that night. To my surprise, Charlie had the outside light on and was waiting for the report that evening—no matter how late I came to the house.

Without Charlie Brook's help I would not have completed my *Meeting and Fishing the Hatches* manuscript. At the time I worked with him, Charlie was ill and didn't fish much. Although he continued to write in his later years, as he got older, Charlie, like all of us, didn't fish as long or as often. I begged him several times to fish with me but he always declined, saying he wasn't feeling well. But he was never too sick to tell me which rivers to fish, what hatches I might see, and to listen to each day's episode.

You might think I complain too much about the two Montana natives who had promised to guide me through my first few days in those strange environs. But remember, until that trip I had never crossed the Mississippi River. So I had to learn the rivers, the geography and the hatches in a couple months on my own and write intelligently about all of those aspects.

I had certainly been abandoned on the first part of that western trip when the two local experts who were to help didn't show up. But Charlie Brooks made up for it. For two weeks, he guided me through every trip and helped me immeasurably. Writing the western section of *Meeting and Fishing the Hatches* was made much more possible through the complete help of this famous fly fishing writer. He helped me because he wanted to and because he's a kindly and helpful person, and for that I am forever indebted to him. Yes, I was alone on the Bitterroot but not for the rest of that first western trip. Charlie Brooks saved the trip and in a great way helped me write my first book.

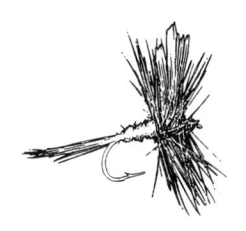

Chapter 7
Black Flies, Gray Skies And Green Drakes

"THIS IDEAL WATER SHOULD BE PROLIFIC of insect life as the heaviest trout will take an interest in surface food when there is a big batch of natural flies, particularly if these are large size.

THEODORE GORDON &
A COMPANY OF ANGLERS
American Trout Fishing

Black Flies, Gray Skies & Green Drakes

THIS WOULD BE A FIRST. I've fished some great and far-off places. Sure, I fished for a month in New Zealand, and yes, I've fished several rivers for trout in Ontario, Canada. But for years, I'd dreamt of huge brook trout in Labrador, one of the last outposts in North America. Would the trip live up to its expectations? Would it be a once-in-a-lifetime trip? Or would it end up as so many promising trips did—a dud? Only time and travel would tell, but my expectations were admittedly high.

Have you ever heard someone say, "You can't get there from here?" They probably referred to fishing some of the more remote locations in Labrador. After we got off our commercial flight in Goose Bay, we had to take another flight to a remote camp 50 miles away. I wondered what would happen if any of the anglers got sick at that isolated camp, with no flight out of the camp for a week.

We arrived much lighter than when we boarded the plane at Newark, New Jersey—once again, the airline left our luggage behind. Once again, we were at an isolated, pristine camp with rivers and lakes surrounding us, teeming with record brook trout and no fishing gear. We didn't have any idea when the gear would catch up with us either. Ed Quigley and Steve McDonald, both southeastern Pennsylvanians, accompanied me. All three of us were without fishing gear. The six other guests at the lodge also had their luggage detained. We would have to wait another day or two until it arrived. Eventually we heard that the airplane was over weight so the airline authority left luggage for 25 people behind.

All dressed up and nowhere to go. Just imagine—twenty-five unhappy anglers, ready to fish at various Labrador camps and no gear. But dedicated anglers are persistent. Our group begged and borrowed some fishing gear for that first evening.

And we were all eager to fish. When we arrived in Goose Bay, Jack and Lorraine Cooper, our hosts for the week, said we were in luck: The great Green Drake of the North had just begun to emerge on the evening we came. We could expect heavy hatches the entire week we spent at the lodge. So much for "you should have been here last week." I could hardly believe it! I finally arrived at a pristine destination precisely when I should have for the best fishing. Wonder of all wonders—the Green Drake would appear every evening we fished.

Our guides for the week were Raymond Best, Chad Snow, Patrick Broomfield, Howard Guptill and Ralph Coles. These men took turns with the guests. Each day we had a new guide, something that benefits both guides and clients.

That first evening Steve McDonald and I had Ralph Coles as our guide. After dinner, he raced out on the lake to a pre-selected spot so we could fish until sunset. As we skimmed across the smooth lake surface, we saw thousands of dazed duns. Cool daytime temperatures, a leaden sky and a fine drizzle brought the hatch on early that evening and prevented all but the hardiest of these large, pale yellow duns from taking flight. Those that escaped the cool water and the cool in the center of the lake had at least nearly half a mile to fly before they were safe, resting on a shoreline vegetation. Some couldn't make the non-stop flight and lighted on the water to rest a second and third time. Many of the stunned yellow duns never took flight again.

I was astonished at the necessary long-distance flight of these mayflies and wondered how any survived the harsh environment—especially on an evening like the one we encountered. They exist here only because each surviving female spinner lays several hundred fertilized eggs. Oddly, I never saw a bird capture any of the dazed or flying duns during the week I spent at the camp. At least these giant mayflies had one less predator to contend with.

The first evening's gray skies were portents of the week ahead. Rainy skies even prevented the plane from landing on the lake when we were scheduled to leave the lodge—not that the extra day wasn't worth it.

Ralph raced our small craft into a protected cove, stopped the motor abruptly and we moved ahead slowly, quietly, without the motor for a hundred feet. Seconds after the motor was silenced, we noted what looked like a heavy riser, but the rise form was unlike anything I have ever seen in 35 years of fishing the hatches. Ten to 20 duns rode

Fishing for giant brookies on the Minipi.

the surface within a foot or two of where the first trout rose. With so many mayflies nearby you'd think that this huge brookie would have stayed motionless and gulped in a number of these in the same area. But it didn't, it sucked in a dun, then moved 20 or 30 feet and took in another dun. Guessing which direction these big brook trout would move was tricky. Correct predictions—infrequent—caught trout.

For several days, this characteristic rise form bothered me: When the Green Drakes of the north emerged, they did so in unbelievable numbers—you might see five duns within a square foot of surface. Why didn't the brook trout stay in one location and sip in all the duns in that area like most other trout?

The third evening on the water clarified the entire puzzle for me. On my very first cast, I hooked a huge fish. It took me deep, then ran for more than 100 feet until it had me well into my backing. I finally turned the fish and got it to within a couple feet of the boat. I thought it was a brook trout, but another look revealed a huge northern pike of about 20 pounds. I brought this behemoth up to the boat before it bit through my five-pound leader. The brook trout question was answered in an instant: Because brook trout share the lake with these other huge predators, they have been conditioned over the years to grab food and run. Those that don't eat on the run become a pike's dinner. A moving target is more difficult to hit.

Only one thing spoiled that fantastic first evening—blackflies. They found me tasty: I had bites on top of bites, more than 30 bites one evening, even with a heavy application of insect repellent. Every day the blackflies bit me—they loved my blood.

That first evening presaged the week ahead: Steve McDonald and I experienced successful fishing each and every night on those lakes. Steve broke the ice during our abbreviated initial evening on the lake by catching a four-pound brook trout. I followed it with another four-pounder. We felt much better now. We could now fish the rest of our stay with much less tension.

That week we hit fantastic rises to Green Drake duns emerging and spinners falling each night—not the same Green Drake so popular in the eastern United States. Both the Green Drake of Labrador (scientists call this one *Hexagenia rigida;* we'll call it the Hex hatch) and the Eastern Green Drake (*Ephemera guttulata*, the Ephemera hatch) are massive as mayflies go. Anglers match both with a Size 6 or 8 hook. The underbellies of both are cream to pale yellow, and both have a slightly greenish olive tint to the top of their bodies. But the Hex prefers much slower water than does the Ephemera. Often you'll find the Hex in ponds and lakes, where Ephemera usually lives in streams and rivers. These two prominent mayflies also appear at different times of the year. The Hex is a late June-early July mayfly, depending on the location; and Ephemera appears from mid-May to mid-June, depending on river location.

We also hit black flies and gray leaden skies much of the time. One unexpected bonus was a sporadic but important hatch of Green Drakes on the surface early in the morning. That week the nine anglers caught more than 135 trout, each over four pounds.

The Minipi River system is geologically unusual. We fished large lakes much of the time; but these lakes flowed into other lakes. Some of the rivers connecting them were only a mile or two long. Small trout inhabited the running waters, and larger trout seemed to prefer the impounded areas.

As far as I know, all but one of the major hatches appear during the daylight hours in Labrador. The only one that consistently emerges at night is the Green Drake. I was initially befuddled by this uncharacteristic routine. Why wouldn't more hatches, especially in the summer, routinely appear in the evening? For example, Brown Drakes appear in the United States at dusk in late May and June. You'll find this same species in Labrador from 2 to 5 p.m. Why? This far north the Brown Drake emerges in late June and early July. Evenings at that time of year can be chancy. Any mayfly appearing at dusk in late June or July might not be able to take flight because of cold temperatures. Late July is the warmest time of the year in Labrador and the Green Drake, appearing as it does in the evening, has a better chance to survive the cool environs.

Nature has also provided another quirky event for the northern Green Drake. Remember those sporadic bonus hatches of early morning Green Drakes? Even if cool evening temperatures killed all the drakes in an evening hatch, the species would survive by those few that delayed their emergence until the daylight hours.

The Green Drake spinner fall was also exciting. As the duns diminished in intensity the spinners of the same species provided an angler's delight. Duns from one night became the following night's spinners, falling on the surface by the thousands.

That last evening, Ray Best guided us and Steve McDonald landed several large trout. It was well past dusk when we decided to head back to camp. Ray picked up one of the huge mayflies resting on the surface, put it to his mouth and ate it, the wings dangling from his lips as he attempted to chew the mayfly. He said it was tasty, and that he understood why the trout enjoyed them. I left the mayfly munching to him. I'd never try one, even on a challenge.

What a fantastic week—great fishing, a great hatch, despite the gray skies and. It turned out to be the trip of a lifetime. I've nearly forgotten pesky black flies and gray skies, but will remember those Green Drakes and those behemoth brook trout always.

Chapter 8
Horses, Pain And Pleading

"THE CREEK, THE VALLEY IT FLOWED THROUGH, and the high country it seeped down from provided whatever spiritual nourishment they needed."

HARRY MIDDLETON
The Earth is Enough

Horses, Pain And Pleading

My son, Bryan learned to fish at an early age. At five years old, he opened the trout season on Harvey's Lake in northeastern Pennsylvania with me. Opening days sometimes weren't pleasant those first few years. I'd get upset with him. Within a few minutes after we began fishing he'd put his rod down and begin tossing stones in the water. Would he ever have the patience to fly fish? But, of course, he grew up. When Bryan was 12, we fished almost every spring and early summer evening on Bald Eagle Creek, a central Pennsylvania trout stream. The daily ritual also included an evening stop at the soft ice cream shop on the way home, a reward for good fishing.

At age 12, he cast a spinner and caught trout better than many twice his age. One evening we hit a spectacular and unexpected hatch of March Browns. Dozens of trout rose to the large cream-colored duns in a dusk feeding frenzy. Bryan cast his Mepps Spinner over those fish for more than half an hour and none struck. You would think that at least he'd accidentally hook one of them. Meanwhile, I cast a lifelike Size 12 March Brown dry fly over five trout and each took the imitation. Bryan kept casting and casting until the hatch ended. He didn't catch any trout on the hardware that night, but that momentous hatch taught him a valuable lesson, and on the way back to the car, he vowed never to use spinners and bait again.

About a year later Bryan, my wife, Shirley, and I attended a Pennsylvania Outdoor Writers Association meeting in Wellsboro, Pennsylvania. On Saturday morning Bryan and I fished the lower end of Cedar Run with about 10 other writers. There, Bryan found a dead trout, well over two feet long. Curious, he dangled his fly over the fish lying in midstream until he hooked it. Maybe a hook, possibly old age, perhaps a predator—it hadn't died long ago. Bryan didn't fish any more that day, but proceeded to proudly carry that five or six pound brown trout around on the stream with him the rest of the morning. Writers attending the conference fished the same stretch of the stream, and when they saw the huge trout, asked Bryan how he caught the large brown. By the end of the morning Bryan had concocted a bizarre story about the way that huge brown surfaced for his pattern.

That same evening at the writer's banquet in Wellsboro, President Wes Bower, commenting on the day's activities, asked 12-year-old Bryan Meck to stand up. Bower introduced Bryan to the guests—seasoned outdoor writers—and he said he caught the largest fish of the day and congratulated him. Wes said the fish measured well over 24 inches long. I looked at Bryan and he looked at me and we both winked. Applause thundered for more than a minute, and Bryan was made the guest of honor—for the moment. After the banquet the group chanced off prizes—including fly reels, line and rods and Bryan walked away with the majority of prizes. How quickly his cheers became boos for taking prizes!

Bryan continued to fly fish through college and beyond. He quickly matured into a competent fly fisher. We continued to compete in a friendly way—but the true competitive spirit wasn't very deep beneath the surface. Several years after his college graduation we took a fishing trip to Upper Canyon Outfitters in Alder, Montana.

We arrived late our first day at the ranch, so we decided to fish the small pond just a hundred yards away, and so did five other ranch guests. Still, we learned something.

With no hatch that day, people weren't catching any trout on the spring-fed pond. Weeds so completely covered its bottom (growing up to within two feet of surface) that a wet fly out of the question—at least for the moment.

Bryan, however, created a solution: He decided to fish a tandem rig, a Patriot dry fly on the surface and a Glow Bug wet fly dropper. He tied the Glow Bug about 18 inches behind the Size 12 dry fly. With this arrangement, the Glow Bug sank and stayed just above the weed tops, where cruising trout could easily see and take the pattern.

It didn't take long. In the next two hours Bryan caught over 20 trout while not one other person fishing caught a single fish—and the fish weren't the only things hooked. Soon everyone was asking to see Bryan's rig, and begging for Glow Bugs. A short time later, others were catching trout and the whole feel of the place changed for the better. At the ranch that evening, Bryan and I tied Glow Bugs for all the guests. Bryan certainly showed me a lesson that evening! The next morning more anglers came to the pond armed with tandem rigs of a dry fly and a Glow Bug, and they continued to catch trout.

In the evening of our second day at the ranch, a tan caddis hatch reigned as the supreme trout catcher. We still were using tandem rigs, this time wet and dry tan caddis imitations. Donna McDonald fished with Bryan and me and caught plenty of trout on a down-wing pattern that copied the caddis. It was one of Donna's first hatch-fishing experiences and she did quite well. Shortly thereafter, it was my turn. I caught one trout on a tan caddis dry fly and another on a tan caddis wet fly fished in tandem—at the same time. Two trout together on a tandem rig turned out to be a tangled mess.

The third day, however—and a horseback ride up the East Fork of the Ruby River—really made the trip interesting. Jake and Donna McDonald decided to take Ken Rictor, Lynn Rotz, Bryan and me to the isolated East Branch of the Ruby. The only way to get there was on horseback, a 10 mile jaunt.

I had no riding experience—and three months earlier, I'd undergone hemorrhoid surgery. Just thinking about the long trek was a pain in the rear—literally. I would have preferred to hike in. But that was out. The mountains were too steep.

Jake tried to select the gentlest horse for me. But, ohhhh…the pain! Each hoof clop jolted my rump into the saddle and brought more pain to my bottom.

Then we came to a gigantic mountain. To reach the river, we had to cross it. The trail there involved several miles of two-foot wide horse paths around sheer cliffs. I just closed my eyes—I didn't want to see what would happen if the horse and I fell. We reached the river valley none too soon. My rear end was killing me—I dreaded the ride back. I only hoped the fishing would be worth it.

As we approached the small river, we saw some down-wings appear just above the surface, causing rise rings from the trout that were feeding on them. Tan caddis emerged on this small branch and a copy of the down wing produced fish all afternoon. However, at 3 p.m., Jake decided it was time to head back. It would take us several hours to traverse the desolate, isolated valley and climb the mountain. The chief difference from the morning ride was the sky. It was clouded over, and as we traveled, we saw areas of threatening weather heading our direction. Eight miles to go. Would we make it before rain fell?

You know what happened next, don't you? Those dark skies opened to reveal a lightning display as bright as the Fourth of July and a horrendous thunderstorm. All seven of us got to witness this from those infernal horses in the middle of a high open meadow. We were drenched in minutes, but the horses, seemingly undisturbed by the dreadful storm, continued on plodding along back to the car. Bryan kept yelling and screaming each time he saw a thunderbolt hit nearby. He must have yelled out at least 10 times.

I couldn't count the number of bolts. I kept my eyes closed. If I was going to die I didn't want to see it. I wanted to be surprised. That storm—that trek—lasted for hours, or at least it seems like it. Then finally, we saw the horse van and the cars off in the distance. Thank God! Deliverance! But my rear end pained me so much I could hardly walk the few feet to the car. Never again, I vowed. I'd stay close to the ranch.

Another morning we fished a section just above the ranch. I tied on an Olive Bead Head Caddis and began casting. For more than an hour, no trout struck that pattern. Meanwhile Bryan, just a hundred feet upriver from me, caught trout after trout. In two hours of intense fly fishing he had landed 12 trout to my measly one fish. The son was showing up his father.

Finally I'd had it. I yelled up to Bryan to ask what fly he was using to catch all those trout. "What did you say?" was the tongue in cheek reply Bryan gave.

"What did you catch those trout on," I yelled again.

Finally, I walked up to Bryan and asked him to show me the fly. He begrudgingly displayed the Bead Head Tan Caddis. Bryan considered the heavy tan caddis hatch the evening before and Donna McDonald's previous success with the pattern, and made a good choice. Ultimately, I lost my pride and asked Bryan for a fly. After a few minutes of begging, he gave in, too. I tied his Tan Caddis patterns on my tippet and in no time was fast to a trout. An hour later, I had landed a dozen fish. What a difference a pattern can make.

I'm often asked if Bryan still enjoys fly fishing. What did you do the day before your wedding—iron out last minute details; check with the flower shop, the restaurant and the church to make certain everything was under control; spend time with your bride? Bryan married Julie Light on October 19, 2002 in Clarence, New York. On October 18, Bryan; Austin Morrow, one of his ushers; his best man Eric Melby; one of his friends who planned to attend the wedding, Bill Mingerell, and I spent the entire day catching big steelhead trout on Eighteen Mile Creek near Buffalo, New York. Many of Bryan's friends love to fly fish. The minister who married Bryan and Julie, Rev. Larry Baird, also fly fishes frequently. In the ceremony, Larry said that Bryan practices catch and release when he fishes, but when he found Julie that practice went out the window. She's a keeper.

Horse and pain…I hope I never have to ride one of those four-legged torture devices again as long as I live. I prefer wheels under me. Pleading? As long as Bryan has a fly I need to match the hatch, the pleading will last as long as I live and continue to fish.

Chapter 9

The Trico Winter

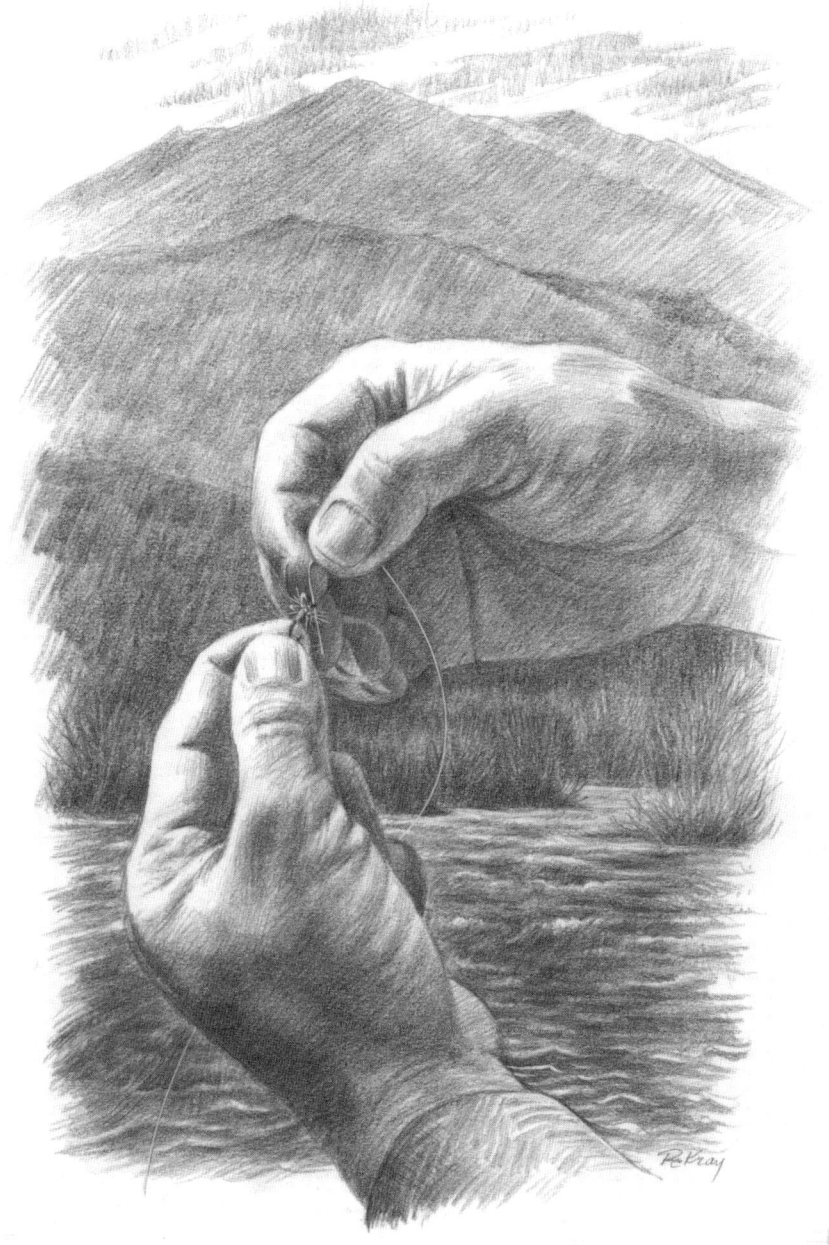

"THE "TINIEST OF MAYFLIES" AND "THE WHITE CURSE" are terms referred to by Vincent C. Marinaro in his 1969 *Outdoor Life* article about these minutae which zoomed this important hatch into national focus. In his report, Mr. Marinaro identified these wee ephemerids with the aforementioned British terms and erroneously called them the "Caenis hatch," instead of the correct Tricorythodes designation. Nevertheless, Mr. Marinaro's accurate account of this activity is accomplished with candor and an intense fervor that conveys his deep feeling for this hatch to the reader."

AL CAUCCI & BOB NASTASI
Hatches II

The Trico Winter

For 15 years, I supervised continuing education workers at seven commonwealth Penn State campuses, a job that kept me in cold winter country. I visited each campus on an average of once a month, traveling to Erie, Sharon, Wilkes-Barre, Scranton and other more remote, snow-prone areas. On several occasions I got stranded in the middle of nowhere because of snow. I once spent an entire week in Titusville, in northwestern Pennsylvania, because a blizzard closed the roads and people couldn't get into or out of town. Involuntarily stuck for a winter week in Titusville is dreary, uninviting—especially that winter, when the snow banks almost reached the telephone wires. (However, Titusville in the spring, summer and fall boasts plenty of nearby trout streams including Thompson, Caldwell, Pine and Oil Creeks. These streams and others hold plenty of trout.)

I was fed up with winter in the Northeast. I hated the weather. With knee-deep or higher snow on the ground, I lost many fishing days. When I took early retirement, part of the pleasure was being able to get away from the drudgery of winter travel—as well as being able to write, speak and fish. But several harsh snow-filled Pennsylvania winters curtailed any winter fishing thoughts. During the winter of 1995-96, for example, 115 inches of snow fell at my central Pennsylvania home while I sat looking out of the windows, dreaming of warmer weather and fishing the hatches. Temperatures in the low teens much of January and February added insult to injury. Add to that 20 straight days of cloudy weather, and you can readily see why I got depressed—seasonal affective disorder, they call it. I had to get out.

So Shirley and I decided to spend our winters in warmer climes. We selected Phoenix, Arizona because the winters were mild, and nearby trout fishing dangled its charms. Trout in the Valley of the Sun? It's true.

Arizona has more than 150 trout streams and some terrific lakes that hold plenty of trout. I'd been in the Grand Canyon state for only a couple of days that first winter when I discovered that just 15 miles from our winter home, I could fish the Salt River for trout instead of suffering snow, sleet and cold in Pennsylvania.

Water is king in the Southwest. During the winter, the Salt River Project conserves much of the Salt River flow for summer use by restricting the flow considerably below Saguaro Lake. In the winter this upper five miles flows at eight or nine cubic feet per second. However, conditions on the lower half of the Salt River are different. Here, after the Verde River enters the Salt, five miles of river holds water aplenty all winter. Arizona also stocks trout on this lower stretch in the winter. Water temperatures in the lower Salt get too warm to hold summer trout. However, the upper end is a tailwater during the summer and does hold trout throughout the year. The secret is to fish the lower five miles in the winter, the upper section in the summer.

Shortly after I arrived in the Valley of the Sun, my son Bryan, and his boss, Todd Coyne, from Astra-Zeneca, joined me for a mid-November morning of Salt River fishing. Bryan and Ted had a meeting in early afternoon in Phoenix, so we only had a couple hours to fish.

Todd asked me about hatches—I assured him we wouldn't see any. I didn't think the river held many insects. We caught a half dozen trout on assorted Zebra Midge patterns tied on a tandem rig. Then about 10 a.m., a huge cloud of small glistening spinners formed in front of us. Tricos!

Was I ever wrong about this hatch! This mid-November Trico spinner was one of the heaviest late hatches I had ever seen. Few of these planted trout rose to the hatch, so we wrote it off as a fluke occurrence.

Two months later, on New Year's morning, I decided to fish the Salt River's lower end—a mile or two downriver from its juncture with the Verde. I hiked the mile from the road to reach the river. There was no path and the last hundred feet was spent crawling through thick brush. For desert country there certainly was a lot of vegetation.

By 9 a.m. on New Year's Day I was fishing under bright blue skies and temperatures that had already climbed past 55 degrees—a typical winter day in the Valley of the Sun.

By 10 a.m. a few small mayflies emerged in some of the slower water in front of me. I assumed they were Little Blue-winged Olives and tied on a Size 18 pattern to match that hatch. Little Blue-winged Olives are very common in the Southwest. I've encountered plenty of these mayflies, even on walks through the middle of Mesa, Arizona.

Trout didn't rise to the emerging duns, though, so I just watched, enthralled by this midwinter hatch and the spectacular weather. Soon the spinners formed a conspicuous mating formation about 10 feet above the surface. It looked oddly like a Trico mating formation. But I didn't think Tricos emerged at this time of year.

Nearby, another angler saw the same phenomenon and, curious about these midwinter spinners in the air, came over to ask what was happening. His name was Virgil Bradford. (We've stayed in touch ever since that episode, even though he has moved several times.)

"What the heck are those little spinners in the air?" Virgil asked.

I said they looked a lot like summer Tricos, but they certainly wouldn't appear this time of the year. I finally captured one of the errant spinners with my fishing cap and examined it. Wonder of wonders—that mayfly was a summer Trico. But here in the Valley of the Sun these small critters experience summer all year long. The water temperatures on the Salt below the lake seldom go below 55 degrees—

even in January. Not one trout rose to the 100 or so spinners that fell that first day of the year so I assumed that this was another aberration.

In mid-February, Craig Josephson and I traveled 90 miles north of Phoenix to Cottonwood. This part of the Verde Valley gets an occasional snowfall, but for much of the winter this area is mild, a great place to live. The state fish and game agency plants trout in the upper Verde throughout the winter. Before we went fishing, I visited with Pete Sesow, Cottonwood's Chamber of Commerce executive director, and asked him where I could find trout. Luckily enough, Pete is an avid fly angler and he told me to try the Dead Horse State Park area just outside town. Pete said that the area gets quite a bit of fishing pressure, but few anglers ever use flies.

Craig, just in from snowy Syracuse, New York, was anxious to get fly fishing. We parked our car at a picnic pavilion, gathered our gear and walked to the river. At 9 a.m. it was already relatively mild—about 50 degrees—and predictions called for a high in the 70s. What a day to fly fish for an East-coaster!

The 40-foot-wide river offered us emerging mayflies immediately. Again, I thought they were Little Blue-wing Olives, the most common species in the Southwest. We tied on patterns to match the emerging mayfly, but nothing happened. No trout rose.

Soon, the problem revealed itself. I saw that familiar Trico spinner formation, and yelled to Craig that they were Tricos. We tore off the Blue-Winged Olive patterns, hurriedly replacing them with smaller Trico spinner imitations. Luckily, I brought some of these midsummer flies with me. By the time the bicolor Trico spinner pattern was on my tippet, the first trout rose. Soon more than 10 more rainbows joined in. Within 15 minutes after the spinners began falling on the surface, Craig and I had pods of more than 20 trout rising in front of us.

Shortly after the first trout took the first spinner, I hooked a small rainbow. Hooking an Arizona trout on a Trico imitation in the middle of the winter was a momentous experience. Few eastern anglers can claim that distinction. The spinner fall lasted for more than two hours and was as heavy as many respectable spinner falls I've seen in midsummer. The fish were taking them, too, more trout rising than I normally see with the best of Trico hatches and spinner falls in August. More than 20 trout took those small Trico spinners that day. That would have been a tremendous day during the normal hatch in the summer—

here, in the middle of winter it was truly spectacular, the most memorable small hatch of my lifetime.

I thought the hatch had to be a quirk of nature, but it wasn't. The hatch reappeared on the same river at the same spot several times in early March. On each occasion I fished the upper Verde River, I met a fantastic spinner fall and rising trout. The hatch was not a fluke. I could now say I had seen Tricos much every month of the year, especially in this winter of Tricos.

Chapter 10

Ten For Ten—
Well, Almost

"THE *BAETIS* SPECIES ARE WITHOUT QUESTION of paramount importance to the angler as they represent a valuable yearround food source for the trout."
AL CAUCCI & BOB NASTASI
Hatches II

Ten for Ten—
══ Well, Almost ══

EVER HEARD OF A BASEBALL HITTER GOING 10 FOR 10? How about a quarterback throwing 10 straight completions? What about a grouse hunter going 10 for 10? How about a fly angler catching or at least hooking 10 trout on 10 casts? Too good to be true, you might say.

Well, it happened to me one day on a small Arizona trout stream with a small nondescript hatch that many anglers would have blown off. Allow me to explain:

Some of the greatest fly fishing I've experienced has come while fishing over hatches of small, unremarkable mayflies; many incidents occurring on days that were less than pleasant—a good number on downright miserable days. I often equate Little Blue-winged Olives with these overcast, cool, drizzly days. Little BWOs are, to me, "the lousy day" hatch. And the moral of the story is that if you fish on a drizzly, overcast, cool day, you should look for these small mayflies. (I wrote about this in *Great Rivers—Great Hatches*, an entire chapter devoted to fishing "lousy" days.)

The Little BWO is found on probably eight of every 10 trout streams in the United States. Yet the Little BWO reigns supreme in the Southwest, an extremely common hatch on just about every stream in New Mexico and Arizona. On Oak Creek near Sedona anglers call this hatch "The Early Blue" because of its color and the fact that it appears most commonly in March and April. You'll even see this mayfly in some of the desert areas of the Southwest. Almost every day in the winter I encounter Little BWOs on the Salt River, just 20 miles from Phoenix.

Heavy hatches of this Little BWOs often take place in areas where you wouldn't expect to see it.

For example, I walk every day. My doctor gave me an ultimatum 30 years ago: Take better care of your health, or die young. I decided to walk, up to 12 miles daily. The other part of my daily routine involves writing from 6–8 a.m. daily, printing out what I have written, then editing the work from 8:30–11 a.m., usually on my walk—I carry a clipboard, reading and making changes, seldom looking at the scenery.

Having escaped central Pennsylvania's sometimes-harsh winters several years ago for Mesa, Arizona—the bonus is great weather, hatches and trout fishing all winter—I've discovered many of the Southwest's rivers hold great winter hatches, particularly the Trico and Little BWO dun.

One winter day in Mesa, Arizona, I was walking along Main Street, reviewing what I had written that morning—an article about Little BWO duns. I'd just started the sentence about how Little BWOs are common, when a small Little BWO spinner landed on the typed page on my clipboard. It clambered across the words "little Blue-winged Olive" for a moment, then twisted its tail in characteristic BWO fashion.

So where did this mayfly come from in the desert, I wondered. Central Arizona has plenty of canals and small lakes crisscrossing the valley. The canals and lakes hold thousands of mayflies—but very few trout. Yet only 15 miles from Mesa I'd encountered fantastic Little BWO hatches and spinner falls and I've seen dozens of trout feeding on them.

In the Southwest water is the golden rule: He who has the water rules. In the winter the Salt River Project preserves every drop of water that enters the watershed. The last barrier to this resource in Mesa is Saguaro Lake. For much of the winter there's a six-mile section below the Saguaro Lake dam that has the minimum mandatory flow of nine cubic feet per second (cfs).

One afternoon, while I fished below the dam, the water was running at more than 100 cfs. We'd had some rain and snowmelt from the mountains that pushed the river high. Certain days of the month—even during the winter—the Salt River Project releases water in the Phoenix area from Saguaro Lake for irrigation. The water flows about seven miles downriver before it reaches Granite Reef. Here the entire flow is diverted into a series of canals that crisscross the Valley of the Sun. The dam's water managers noticed the high water and shut the dam gates. Almost instantaneously, the water went down to the minimum and wet banks became dry, and rocks previously covered with water were soon exposed. Shortly, thousands of Little BWOs emerged

The Little Blue-winged Olive dun.

from the now dry spots—a phenomenon I had never seen before. If they didn't they would have died.

The Southwest's Little BWO hatches appear throughout the winter. The best time to see Phoenix's hatches is January and February. About 150 miles northeast of Phoenix these same small mayflies appear on some of Arizona's better trout streams in late fall, and the very early spring. Local anglers call them The Early Grays. Some of the better hatches in the northern half of the Grand Canyon state occur in February, March and April. One of the best Little BWO hatches I ever hit in the Southwest occurred in mid-April near the recently fire-scarred town of Show Low, in north-central Arizona.

I was working on *Arizona Trout Streams and Their Hatches* at the time, and had just two weeks to complete the manuscript. Terrible winter weather in the high mountains set me back several weeks, necessitating a begrudged deadline extension.

Deep snows prevented me from reaching several rivers I wanted to cover for the book. I still had 20 streams in the Mogollon Rim area to cover. (When I tell anglers outside Arizona that there are more than 150 trout streams in that state they are amazed. One reason trout streams are found in this area is the Mogollon Rim. It rises 6,000- 10,000 feet above the desert floor, creating a water trap that sends moisture to the valleys below.) Snow or not, the deadline prompted a trip to fish Silver Creek, near Show Low.

It was mid-April, yet the skies over Silver Creek were a battleground. Snow squalls disputed territory claimed by Spring's cobalt clearness much of that afternoon. Suddenly, the blue sky would grow dark and a heavy coating of white fell on the stream's banks. Then the leaden clouds would retreat, routed by a gusty charge of the bright Arizona blue. The weather just couldn't make up its mind.

Virgil Bradford, Brian Williams and I met near Show Low. Most of Arizona's trout waters are put-and-take, often stocked with trout for the spring and summer months. Silver Creek was no exception. Even though this spring-fed stream holds a trout hatchery at its upper end, it still depends on stocked trout. The three of us visited the hatchery that cold, early spring morning and asked the workers when they planned to stock the lower end. They told us that they planned to plant a few hundred trout in the stream below that same afternoon, so we thought we'd watch them stock and see what happened. About 2 p.m., the workers appeared and the three of us kidded each other about following the stocking truck.

Within minutes of the stocking, a heavy Little BWO hatch appeared on the surface. Cold early spring temperatures delayed any but the hardiest of these tiny mayflies from taking flight. To our amazement, the freshly-planted trout began taking dazed duns off the surface. I can't explain it, but these trout seemed to know they could no longer depend on hatchery food. In front of us, more than 30 of those recently planted trout fed freely off the surface.

This was one of Brian's first fly fishing adventures, and he got anxious when he saw all those trout taking food off the top. He asked me what fly he should use, and I gave him a Vernille-bodied Little BWO dun, a pattern Bill Howe of Huntingdon, Pennsylvania claims to have created, while Virgil and I tied on more conventional parachute patterns with dubbed olive bodies.

I sat back, watching Brian for a while, coaching him on his presentation. On the very first cast with that pattern Brian missed a trout. On the second cast he missed another one. On the third cast he hooked and released his first trout. Brian caught, hooked or missed 10 trout in his first 10 casts.

Those freshly-planted trout fed on Little BWO duns and slurping that Size 20 Vernille-bodied dry fly from the surface with abandon. Upstream, Virgil Bradford had the same kind of success.

Enough was enough! I wanted to participate, not be a spectator. I headed below Brian and began casting to a pod of newly-introduced risers. One after another those rainbows took our imitations. I'm convinced that much of our success and the intensity of the hatch can be attributed to the inclement weather we experienced that day. Cold water and air kept those insects from taking flight. We ended up catching more than 30 trout on dry flies—all rising to a seemingly unending supply of Little BWOs. The cold shortened our fishing trip, but we were satisfied that we had just hit an unbelievable hatch and triumphantly matched it.

When he's not fishing or hunting Brian is a dentist in Mesa. Every time I see him in his office, I look at him and he looks at me and one of us blurts out, "10 for 10—well, almost." We'll remember that cold blustery day on Arizona's Silver Creek and its Little Blue-winged Olive hatch for the rest of our lives—despite the trout being recently planted fish. Going 10 for 10 is a rare occurrence, whether it's baseball, football or grouse hunting—even fly fishing—especially for someone just starting out.

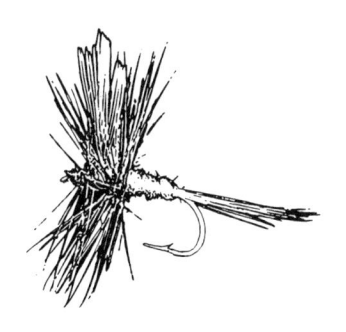

Memory Rising

Hatches, Waters & Trout

"Memory Rising"
Original Acrylic
Robert Clement Kray © 2003

Original Art & Photographs

"Leaper"
Original Acrylic
Robert Clement Kray © 2003

"Steelhead"
Original Acrylic
Robert Clement Kray © 2003

"Brown Trout"
Original Acrylic
Robert
Clement Kray ©
2003

Sulphurs

Above—*Spring Creek's (Pa.) Sulphur duns figured heavily in "That'll Catch Trout."*

Below—*The real thing...*

New Zealand

Left—*The Worsley River.*

Above—*The Black Caddis pattern that hammered New Zealand trout.*

Right—*Mike Manfredo with a South Island fish.*

Above— *Fishing South Island's Wyndham River.*

Right— *Mistake Creek's pristine waters don't appear to be in any error.*

Great Memories

*The author, **left**, will never forget the Pale Morning spinner fall on the Bighorn River. On this great river, a fantastic hatch and a good guide yielded one of his best memories.*

Tricos

Below—*A female Trico spinner. Triocs gave angling legend Vince Marinaro fits one day on Falling Spring Creek (Pa.).*

Right—*Bowman Creek, where Meck and Ray Thomas frequently fished, and where Marinaro redeemed himself as Trico Master.*

THE HATCH OF A LIFETIME

Above—*A Blue Quill, which brought trout up for the group on Bobs Creek and Spruce Creek in Pennsylvania.*

Left—*Andrew Goldman was Vice President Dick Cheney's assistant when Meck shared some of southcentral Pa.'s best waters with Cheney and friends. After just a few minutes of instruction, Goldman landed a Spruce Creek trout.*

Above—*Helping other anglers catch trout is part of what drives Meck. Here, Evan Morse lands a nice trout.*

Minipi Brook Trout

Above—Steve McDonald shows a large brook trout he caught on the Minipi.
Right—Fishing for giant brookies on the Minipi.
Above—Canada's gray skies often yielded spectacular sunsets.

The Intuder

Above—Evan Morse lands a small trout taken on a White Fly.

Left—The real thing: a White Fly.

Below—Anglers fishing Yellow Breeches Creek in Pennsylvania during the White Fly hatch.

Trout West

Above—*The Verde River's midwinter flow is often low.*

Left—*Brian Williams holds one of 10 trout he caught in a row.*

Below—*A Little Blue-winged Olive dun.*

Above—*Bryan Meck lands a Ruby River trout. His father suffered a long—and painful—horseback ride to reach these fish.*

Left—*The North Platte River in Wyoming has a great White Fly hatch.*

Below—*The Kootenai River, host to a Pale Morning Dun hatch.*

Above—*Anglers line the banks of the San Juan River in New Mexico.*

Right—*A Missouri River trout...*

Left—*Fishing the North Fork of the Cache la Poudre.*

THE GREEN DRAKE

Above—*Fishing for rising trout in Penns Creek during a Green Drake hatch.*

Right—*A Green Drake natural...*

Above—*A bead-head Pheasant Tail nymph...*

Right—*Former Miami Dolphin running back Larry Czonka (in brown shirt on left) and Meck discuss strategy during a television show filming.*

THEY'RE TRYING TO KILL ME!

Above—*Tennessee's Abrams Creek was hard-won access. Meck thought he wouldn't make it up the steep bank, through the laurel.*

Left—*Another look at Abrams Creek. Lots of rocks...*

Above—*The Blue-winged Olive*

Left—*Austin Morrow, ESPN host, lands a trout.*

Secret Streams

Above—*Paul Weamer enjoys fishing his secret stream.*

Right—*Autumn trout fishing along a secret stream.*

Chapter 11
The Intruder

"Then came that loud splash and the water beside the rock began to boil as if it were on high heat."

Harry Middleton
The Earth is Enough

The Intruder

One of summer's last hatches, the White Fly, is a harbinger, a sign that fall can't be too far away, that winter is just around the corner. White Fly hatches are happenings. White Flies appear in a very short time and are highly concentrated, a hatch that crowds covet and one that can provide plenty of good memories. This hatch summons plenty of trout to the surface as well as angling hordes to those streams and rivers with this insect. One is a natural outgrowth of the other.

White Flies, like Tricos, have an unusual life cycle. Like the Trico, within minutes after they've emerged from beneath the surface, White Flies are ready to mate and lay their eggs. Then the duns fall spent on the surface, the cycle continuing for another year. Once the female deposits her fertilized eggs, they lay dormant until the following spring. I find it amazing that these small creatures spend only minutes above the surface breeding and laying eggs, and almost a year under water as an egg and nymph.

White Flies are trout manna. Trout go crazy during a White Fly hatch, schlepping bugs off the surface like pellets in a hatchery. The hatch usually appears in mid- to late August, begins around 7:30 or 8 p.m. and continues for an hour. The fish gorge themselves on dead and dying duns and spinners every evening during the White Fly hatch, which usually lasts about a week.

White Fly hatches are both blessings and a curse. The blessing is the influence of the hatch on trout, how the trout feed on this hatch. The curse is two-fold: The crowds are one part of it, the other is that the White Fly represents one of the final hurrahs of the trout fishing season. For many, this hatch will be the last hatch of the season, a conclusion that signals anglers to hang up their gear for the winter.

I hate fishing heavily-fished streams. Some say—with much credibility—that I shouldn't complain, because I'm the one who has caused these crowded waters by writing about them. For some of this I will take responsibility. On occasion, I've seen anglers parked near areas I have written about with a copy of my book on their seat. Near one of my favorite Pennsylvania streams, I noticed a vehicle with an Oklahoma license plate with a copy of my book on the seat. I complained about that Oklahoma truck—until I saw my book on his front seat.

But streams and rivers need friends. The more anglers who fish a stream, the more friends that particular stream has, and the more people who will eagerly defend and protect that precious resource. Look at polluted streams that hold no trout. Who cares about them? But a stream that holds a good trout population, is frequented by many anglers, is a stream or river people want to protect. The more anglers who fish the stream, the more advocates the stream has to preserve and protect it, should something happen.

Those desiring a White Fly experience should visit Pennsylvania—particularly the Susquehanna River near Harrisburg, or Yellow Breeches Creek in Boiling Springs. You'll see what I mean by crowded conditions. Hundreds of anglers fish the river near Harrisburg when fish rise to White Flies during late July and August. Smallmouth bass are the main focus, but catfish and other species of fish gorge themselves on an almost unending supply of food. It's nature's way of preparing these fish for slim pickings during winter. While fishing for bass on the Susquehanna I've caught some huge channel catfish. Until you've seen it, you wouldn't believe it, but those huge catfish feed on these critters on the surface. Just a few miles away, near Boiling Springs, on Yellow Breeches Creek, the hatch appears around the middle of August. Here, anglers fish the hatch over a good number of rising trout.

Yellow Breeches has enormous crowds when the White Fly appears. It's like a carnival, like 10 opening days rolled into one: Fly anglers meet in the parking lot about 5 p.m. to plan strategies. Slowly, the stream fills with people, each beat becomes occupied. People, standing almost elbow-to-elbow, talk and wait until the hatch finally appears, then a quiet, punctuated by the swish of fly line through guides, sweeps over the stream as the anglers cast to rising trout. The yelling starts when anglers hook up with one of the risers—"got one!" or "damn!" This goes on for an hour or two until the hatch wanes and the skies darken.

Evan Morse lands a small trout taken on a White Fly.

Andrew Krouse and Craig Josephson both know this hatch. They've seen the crowds and fished the water. New White Flies will predictably reappear on the same stretch the next night, which means another chance at a lunker.

For years, I've put up with this crowded stream nonsense, but I finally go tired of it. Such disparate waters as the Little Juniata River in central Pennsylvania and the North Platte River in southern Wyoming also hold the White Fly about a week or two later than the one on the Yellow Breeches. Fishing a little later on a less popular river for the hatch can provide a less crowded chance at hungry fish.

I first discovered the White Fly hatch on the Little Juniata River about 12 years ago. The Little Juniata has experienced many down years since that time. If left alone, this river is one of the tops in the nation. But civilization and humans have treated this fertile limestone water harshly. Over the years, various spills have had a detrimental effect on the river's trout and its insects. Most recently, during 1996, high water in January washed insecticides into the river, nearly destroying the hatches. Where Sulfurs and White Flies once reigned supreme, few were seen for several years. However, the waterway is recovering.

I invited John Randolph, editor of *Fly Fisherman* magazine, and Jim Hawthorne along to fish the hatch 12 years ago. John is a devoted fly angler who enjoys experiencing hatches on a variety of waters. His well-received book, *Becoming a Fly Fisher*, lucidly shares some of his White Fly experiences during the past two decades on the Susquehanna River. John had only seen the White Fly on Yellow Breeches and the Susquehanna before that evening. Jim Hawthorne, at the time, lived just a few miles from the river and fished the Little Juniata almost daily. (Jim has since become a professional Madison River fly fishing guide, working out of Sheridan, Montana. I won't forget the big smiles on the faces of two nuns I met at the Upper Canyon Outfitters in Alder, Montana, who had just spent a day with Jim. Jim really delivered for these ladies. They had never fly fished before and he made sure they caught some Madison River trout.) That evening on the Little Juniata, John, Jim and I caught plenty of trout during the White Fly hatch. We fished until well after dark and used a flashlight to work our way back to the car.

Word of mouth brought far too many anglers to the "Little J's" White Fly hatch. With dozens of anglers appearing on the river as regularly as the White Fly, I soon had enough of the crowds here, too. I hunted for areas of the river where I could find wide open spaces and solitude. Several years of searching finally resulted in my finding a real White Fly Mecca. Just to prove it to myself, I fished it solid for a week. During that time, it showed me copious White Fly hatches every evening, not another angler, and the final ingredient for a perfect hatch, plenty of rising trout.

On Saturday evening, I came back to this stretch of the stream, looked up and down the river, and couldn't see a solitary angler for half a mile in either direction. I was in luck!

The hatch began early that evening—by 7 p.m. male spinners, some still carrying their pellicle behind them, raced up and down river searching for females. More males joined the spinners, already in their mating flight, and then the females emerged. The air was filled with white mayflies moving up and down on the river. The trout certainly noticed. Within minutes, rise rings plopped up everywhere. I had more than 20 trout feeding within casting distance.

Under those circumstances, choosing which fish to cast to first became the question—what a treat! These trout took my imitation on almost every flawless cast. They were easy pickings. Once I even dragged the pattern and a feeding brown nailed it.

After about the fourth trout, though, I heard car doors slamming. About 100 yards behind me, I heard talking. Then five anglers waded into the stream behind me. I thought there was plenty of room up and down the river, so these gents wouldn't crowd me. But was I ever wrong. The quintet waded right towards me; two anglers went above, three just below me. The empty river suddenly seemed so full, so much like Pennsylvania's opening day trout hoopla.

They waded nearer, crowding me. I looked up to the sky, gave a little prayer and said if there's a God up there, I deserve to catch one trout while they were getting rigged up. There must be, because my prayer was quickly answered with a saucy, 17-inch brown trout. I released the fish while the five sports knotted tippets and got ready to cast. They started talking, then cast in the direction of some risers. I'd had enough—I didn't come for a crowd. I wound up my line and waded back out of the stream and to the car. I gave up. They won—they got me out of the water. Evidently I had been fly fishing their favorite stretch and they were determined to get me out of there. They succeeded. A few years later, I wrote about how I felt about this unpleasant incident in *Patterns, Hatches, Tactics and Trout*. Larry Seaman, the book's illustrator, even created art that reflects getting crowded in.

Almost 12 years to the day after this incident, I was signing books at McFarland Rod Company's grand opening in Bellwood, Pennsylvania, a favor for Mike McFarland. When my talk and the signing was over, one man remained in the rear, sheepish, staring in my direction, as though he had something to say.

I was wrapping things up when he approached me, saying that he was one of the five who had crowded me that evening on the Little Juniata River. He had read my perspective on this in my book, and wanted to give me his side of the story. Turns out he wasn't a bad guy. He told me that he and his friends had come up from New Jersey to trailer camp and fish half a mile upstream from "my" White Fly hotspot every year for the last five years. I was the first angler they had seen there in almost a year. And they felt like they "owned" that water, too; that I was the intruder.

I visited with this gentleman shortly after meeting him at McFarlands. I even gave him some new patterns to try on the river. Those anglers had as much right to that portion of the river as I did. And it felt good to soothe any bad blood between us, to be a gentleman. Rivers belong to themselves, not to those who try to possess them, and perhaps we both learned a lesson on that.

Chapter 12
The Upside-Down Drakes

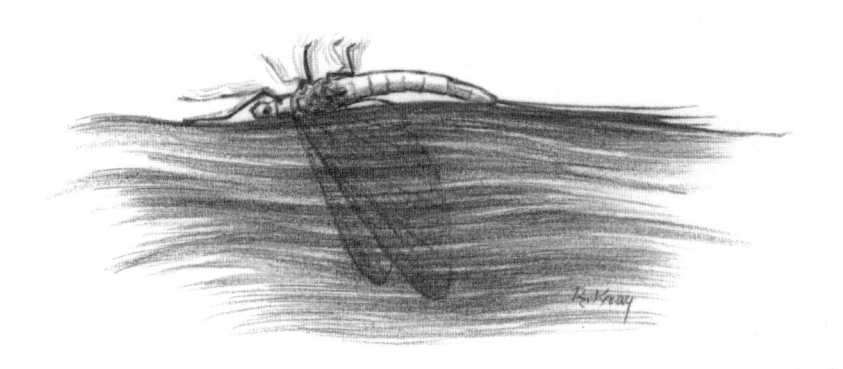

"[Ephemera] Guttulata is one of the largest and most spectacular mayflies in the Eastern U.S."

Al Caucci & Bob Nastasi
Hatches II

The Upside-Down Drakes

I'VE SEEN MY SHARE OF BIZARRE HATCHES in my lifetime: I've hit fantastic January and February Trico hatches on Arizona's waters. I've witnessed one of my most successful Western Green Drake hatches just below Colorado's Reudi Reservoir on the Fryingpan River in early September, well after that hatch should have ended for the year. (I caught huge rainbows feeding on those drakes as late as Labor Day.) I've seen little black stoneflies crawling on snow banks along Arizona's Tonto Creek in February, and huge rainbows feeding on tiny midges as early as March and April on the Cache la Poudre River in Colorado in early April—and in Arizona, at Lee's Ferry on the Colorado River, in March. Yet none of these strange happenings comes close to an event three of us witnessed on central Pennsylvania's Little Juniata River more than 30 years ago. I am still haunted by that hatch, the natural mystery surrounding that evening, each time I fish the Little Juniata.

Plenty of rivers have returned from bouts with pollution, and the Little Juniata River is one of those proud examples. For years, the river had raw sewage, tannic acid and other pollutants flowing through its waters. Low water quality thwarted most hatches, yet old-timers claimed the river still held a few behemoth trout, despite the lack of a food supply.

Beginning in the late 1960s, communities built sewage plants and promoted laws that demanded stricter water quality regulations. The result was much cleaner rivers, including the Little Juniata. What was once was a tannic acid-colored, highly-polluted river became a clean, clear, cool stream with plenty of trout in just a few short years.

I first began fishing the river in 1972, shortly after Hurricane Agnes. Rain fell continuously during the storm (June 21 – 26) resulting in more than 12 inches of rain in less than a week. In one sense, all this rain benefited the river. It scoured the bottom and cleansed the waters of pollutants, diluting and washing the contaminants downstream. The flood also washed a trout hatchery from the famous limestone tributary Spruce Creek downstream into the "Little J." Many of these trout were now free, living in the Little Juniata.

In late July, a month after Agnes' flooding had subsided, Mark Davis, a Little Juniata fishing veteran, took me with him to fish the river. Davis' stories of lunker trout caught, even when the river held pollution, tantalized me.

My first view of the Little J was impressive. The river looked clean, the midsummer water temperature was 65 degrees, and the water's surface was teeming with insects. That evening hundreds of Light Cahills dotted the water, and Mark and I caught more than 20 trout on a Size 12 imitation. Many of these trout came from the hatchery upstream on Spruce Creek, the famous limestone stream, and ranged from 12 to 18 inches long. What an evening we had! I vowed to return to these waters, and did, a number of times.

Eleven months later, on the first day of June in 1973, Dick Mills, Jack Conyngham and I returned for an evening on the Little Juniata. All of us were fellow Wilkes-Barre fly tying class alumni and frequent fishing partners—we had spent many days fishing the Beaverkill and Willowemoc in the Catskills, and the North Mountain Club, one of northeastern Pennsylvania's premier private trout clubs. I wanted to show my friends the quality of the fishery, especially the great hatches—Sulfurs, White Flies, Light Cahills, Yellow Drakes, even an occasional late May Green Drake—I had experienced on the river. On the best Green Drake evenings, I'd spot half a dozen Coffin Fly spinners in the air. For a week or more I noticed these spinners mating in very limited numbers.

Jack, Dick and I began our evening on the Little Juniata a mile downstream from where Spruce Creek enters the river on a section at Espy's farm. (A private fishing club now owns this section.) Water temperatures were perfect, in the low- to mid-60s. We had fished for an hour, catching some nice browns on a variety of patterns when something changed, quickly, dramatically.

Little Juniata River.

It began with a few giant Green Drake mayflies appearing on the water's surface. A few minutes later, the water in front of us was covered with fluttering duns. Looking upriver, I saw the entire surface of the pool covered with moving mayflies. Jack, Dick and I tied on large Green Drake patterns and waited for the trout to rise. We waited, and waited, and waited. Half an hour passed, but no trout rose. Why, I wondered?

One oddity was that every Green Drake that emerged did so upside down, their bellies pointed skyward, back facing the water. I don't think I saw more than one or two of the thousands of drakes that emerged right themselves and fly away. It was the most unusual hatch I had ever witnessed, thousands of fluttering, upside-down duns trying to right themselves, yet not one trout coming up to feed on them. I could only stare, mesmerized by this bizarre hatch, and wonder what caused it.

The hatch didn't last very long—we'd waited half an hour for trout to rise—and the three of us went away puzzled. Why did all the mayflies emerge upside down? This curious hatch remained with me for several years while I tried to figure out the mystery.

A review of the Little Juniata's early 1970s history and a study by entomologist Greg Hoover on Penns Creek's Green Drakes done near the same time came close to answering the riddle.

Hoover discovered that Penns Creek nymphs live in burrows for two years before they emerge. Eggs laid this year will emerge as duns 727 days—two springs—later, living above the surface for just a couple of days awaiting for the right opportunity and time to mate. This life cycle has gone on for millions of years. During the nymph's underwater period, it sheds its outer skin many times to accommodate growth.

Spruce Creek, which enters just a mile upriver from where we fished, has a fantastic Green Drake hatch. That hatch and the egg-laying usually occur around May 25. Hurricane Agnes' mid-June flooding dislodged the one-year-old Green Drake nymphs from their burrows in Spruce Creek, and the high water washed the nymphs downriver until they came to a slower section of the Little Juniata River—where Dick, Jack and I fished that evening. There, these displaced nymphs created new homes in the river. They stayed there for a year before they emerged. Evidently this displacement—from the environs of Spruce Creek to the Little Juniata River—disoriented these mayflies enough to make them emerge upside down. It's the only plausible deduction I've come up with in the 30 years since that episode. The nymphs were interrupted in their development and moved to a new location. (Remember how Charles Wetzel's *Trout Flies* discussed his failures at trying to transplant Green Drake nymphs? Later, when he collected a cage full of duns and spinners and released them, his experience proved much more successful. It's something to consider if you're trying to establish a population of mayflies not presently on a stream or river.)

I came back to the same section of the river three evenings after the three of us fished it, looking for more duns to emerge and to see if any spinners fell. I saw neither. I frequently fished the same general area during the next two years in late May to look for more Green Drakes. None appeared, however. Every year the Little Juniata River had just a few Green Drakes appear—until 1988.

On May 26, 1988, an angler called me and said he hit a fantastic Green Drake hatch on the river just two miles below where I experienced that unusual event in 1973. From 1988 until 1995, I hit spectacular Green Drake hatches on the river. The Little Juniata had a following of Green Drake anglers that increased as the hatch became better known. In January of 1996 though, another devastating flood hit the river—spilling chemicals into the river.

Biologists studied the spill for years and still haven't determined what it was, but the pollutant wiped out the Green Drake population and many other hatches.

For several years the river held trout, but they all looked emaciated, the victims of scarce food resources. It will take years to return the Green Drake to its prominence. But with a chapter of the Federation of Fly Fishers and the Little Juniata River Association serving as guardians for the river, the future looks brighter. (Both groups could use your support.)

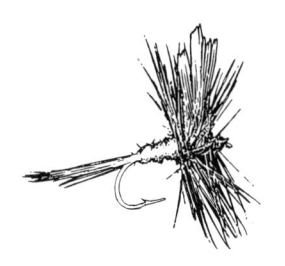

Chapter 13
You'll Never Make It...

"THEY DID NOT BEWAIL their fate and damn the human race."

          HARRY MIDDLETON
          The Earth is Enough

You'll Never Make It

If you're approaching retirement age, you're familiar with the routine: Count the number of days you have to go before retirement, especially when you reach age 62. But I was 54 and I had a deep, dark secret. For the past two years I had kept a confidential calendar with the number of days to go before my early retirement, a secret calendar locked in a drawer in my desk. I wanted out—while I still had time to write. I didn't share that calendar with anybody because I didn't want the word to get out early. Only my wife knew about my future plans.

When the day to tell my boss about my retirement plans arrived—a couple months prior to the actual date—I thought I was ready. For years before that time I had geared up for retirement. I planned to write articles and books about the outdoors, to follow up on the success of *Meeting and Fishing the Hatches*, written nine years earlier.

The time came to give notice, and to share my feelings and my future plans with my boss at Penn State University. I walked into his office one Monday morning and told him I planned to retire in two months. He sat there, stunned for a minute or two, unable to come up with the right words. He just stared at me, his mouth agape. "You're too young to retire," John finally said. "What are you going to do with the rest of your life?"

When I told him I hoped to write several books he looked at me in amazement and said, "You'll never make it."

That's all he said—no congratulations, no best wishes. Those words of his became a rallying cry for me and I never forgot them. In fact, they might just have been what I needed to make me prove to him that he was wrong. Maybe, just maybe, he said those words to challenge me—but whatever his motive in saying them, they lit a fire under me. I probably have thought of those four words every day since then.

Retiring at 54 had its costs. I had to wait eight years for my first Social Security payment. My monthly retirement check from the university was less than $1,000. We still had a mortgage to pay. I had to write and sell my writing, or we wouldn't eat.

When I retired in September, I immediately bought a computer. I had never touched a computer before. I didn't even know how to put the diskette in the darned thing. My wife had to show me how to do that—a learning experience. But I was determined to learn—and to write—spurred on by the words of my boss.

Where would I start? What book would I write? Why not write a book on Pennsylvania trout streams? I've lived my entire lifetime in Pennsylvania, and as a Regional Director of Continuing Education, I covered many areas of the state. On just about every one of those trips, my fishing gear accompanied me. I stayed overnight on many occasions and spent many evenings on Commonwealth waters—and I kept detailed records of every fishing trip and every hatch I'd seen since 1968. Those records and my many fishing trips would help me document the book.

Clyde Johnson, Director of Continuing Education at the Mont Alto Campus during the 1970s and 1980s will tell you, if you ask him, what outfit I wore the first time I came to his office. I had stopped at Falling Springs, a trout-rich limestone stream near Chambersburg and just a couple miles from the campus, fished for an hour and I stopped in the office wearing hip boots. What a way to make an impression on you fellow worker!

On another trip—this one to northeastern Pennsylvania—I stopped at Bowman Creek for an hour of fishing before a scheduled teacher registration. Drivers passing over the bridge just upstream from me stared at the strange fisherman in full regalia—a long sleeved shirt, a tie and a suit coat. The Brits would have been proud of me. I did land a 20-inch brown trout on a Slate Drake that evening. Leaving a hatch of Slate Drakes to make it to the teacher registration—I'm a stickler for time—was hard. Uncharacteristically, I arrived at the Tunkhannock High School meeting 10 minutes late, thanks to that darned late September hatch.

I first sent part of the proposed manuscript for the Pennsylvania book to a large New York publisher. He liked the book idea, but felt that it lacked wide appeal—too regional—and suggested I contact Countryman Press in Vermont with the idea. Carl Taylor, the publisher at Countryman Press, liked the proposal and told me to go ahead with the book. I had no idea what I was in for. I had no idea how long and how detailed the book would be. Part of it was my problem with detail since I wanted to include a comprehensive hatch chart for each stream I covered. I think that was a first in fly fishing literature.

How would I be able to detail the hatches on the 125 waters I planned to cover? I contacted many angler friends I'd gotten to know over the years. Each of these local experts helped me with the hatches. It took an entire fishing season to complete the manuscript for *Pennsylvania Trout Streams and Their Hatches*, and I fished a lifetime of fantastic hatches compacted into that one short fishing season. Imagine fishing for 159 straight days, from March 25 until August 31, even when it rained and the waters were high and muddy. I saw more than 100 hatches, many quite spectacular. My fishing license was a real value that year! I had help on just about every stream I fished. I also took more than 50 rolls of black and white film and 30 rolls of color slides. The book would have taken several years without the help of more than 60 fellow anglers.

Tom Crawford of Falls Creek, Pennsylvania helped with some streams in the northwestern part of the state. We agreed to meet and fish Red Bank Creek one Saturday afternoon. I wanted to interview Tom on the way to and from the stream, and we agreed to meet at 1 p.m. in DuBois' Holiday Inn. I waited and waited for Tom, but he didn't show. At 2 p.m., I called his home and his wife told me he was cutting his lawn. When he finally reached the phone I asked if he was going fishing with me today. He said, matter of factly, that he would, and came to the motel to meet me.

We left for the stream at 3 p.m., and Tom didn't say a word about why he was late, why he didn't show up. We'd quit fishing about 9 p.m., and headed back to the Holiday Inn, when he finally began to tell me why he was late for our fishing trip.

Some of his fellow teachers played unbelievable pranks on each other. One teacher, dressed as hospital personnel, walked in on his wife and pretended he was taking her temperature. When I originally called him at home, he was certain it was just another teacher prank, and he wasn't going to fall for it. "No way Charlie Meck would want me to go fishing with me," Tom said. A teacher and consummate fly fisher, Tom has since retired but still fly fishes passionately.

A few months before the book's publication date, another book, *Pennsylvania Trout and Salmon Guide*, by Mike Sajna, hit the market. My publisher Carl Taylor called me one day and asked how Mike's book would affect sales of my book. I told him that I felt our book would do well because of the hatch charts listed for each stream. Little did I know how well the book would sell.

Many people feel that writers get paid too much. Not so—we're generally underpaid. I received 49 cents a copy for the first 5,000 copies of that book. That's $2,500 for the first printing. My 11,000-mile travel and research expenses were more than $12,000. The average fly-fishing book sells about 6,000 copies, so you're not going to get rich on royalties for that number of books. When the publisher asked me to update and expand the book in 1992, I asked for—and got—more money.

Pennsylvania Trout Streams came on the market on September 25, 1989. I knew we had a popular book on our hands when Carl Taylor called me on December 4, 1989 and told me the book had completely sold out, so quickly that the publisher didn't have a chance to order a second printing before the stock ran out. Carl said that I made Christmas a happy one for the employees of Countryman Press. No one had any copies of my book for the Christmas season. What to do now? Some wanted copies for Christmas presents. I had dozens of calls at my home from people begging for copies. I had 20 copies in reserve but I gave them to Flyfisher's Paradise, the local State College fly shop. The shop has sold more than 1,000 copies of the book since it came out in 1989.

The second printing of the book came out on January 25, 1990. On that day I had scheduled an autograph session at the Evening Rise in Paradise, Pennsylvania, just outside Lancaster's Pennsylvania Dutch Country. Nick and Beverly Delle Donne operated the store. I didn't feel good about a book signing in the dead of winter. I always wonder if anybody will show up. I was certain that few anglers would venture out on that cold, brisk late-January Saturday. A block from the store, I saw a crowd of people outside waiting in a line. I wondered what store had a special and what could entice this many people to remain outside in line on a cold winter day.

Guess what? That long line of people led right to the door of The Evening Rise. They were people waiting for me to sign their books. Wow!

The second printing of the book sold out completely in a month, by February 25, 1990, and it has continued to sell through three editions, sixteen printings and more than 50,000 copies.

In March of 1990, I scheduled more than forty autograph sessions around the state. I came down with a fever and flu symptoms and had to cancel several appearances. At the time, I didn't charge for these appearances at sporting goods stores. Only one of those 40 offered me any money to cover my expenses. While each trip to autograph books cost me at least $50, I only received a few bucks six months later in royalties. When I grew more ill, I decided to cancel all of these free appearances for two weeks because my doctor diagnosed my illness as Chronic Fatigue Syndrome and told me to rest. You wouldn't believe how upset these stores became.

As soon as the book came on the market, book reviewers espoused its merits. One of the first reviews of the book (from a New York newspaper) really sticks in my memory. The review began "I estimate that Charlie Meck is 125 years old." He had no idea how I got all the information I incorporated into the book.

Retirement…sitting back and relaxing? No more deadlines like those I had at Penn State University? You gotta be kidding! Since *Pennsylvania Trout Streams*, I've written 10 additional books. Even so, "You'll never make it" still drives me to write.

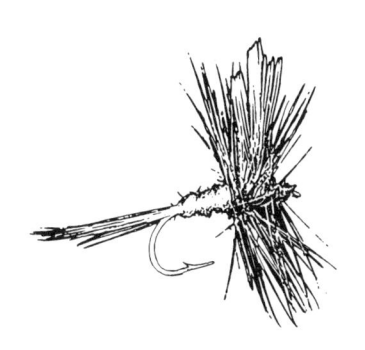

Chapter 14
The Once-In-A-Lifetime Hatch

"Trout fishing at its best is a gentle art, both humbling and satisfying. Many who pursue it never see the subtle side at all, but those who do are never without rich memories and the deep satisfaction that comes with anything well done."

Ernest G. Schweibert
Matching the Hatch

The Once-In-A-Lifetime Hatch

WHAT IS A ONCE-IN-A-LIFETIME FLY FISHING EVENT? Some anglers might dream of an entire day of matching the hatch, the action never letting up, with hundreds of trout rising in front them. And—best of all—you've got precisely the right fly, and plenty of them, so you can replace flies that became tattered from having to release oh so many trout. What a hardship.... (I'm joking of course!) But here's a thought-provoker: What would you do if this actually occurred? People have been known to do strange things under such circumstances. Even if it lasts just five hours. File this under "Charlie's Believe-it-or-Not," but it happened to me on Penns Creek on July 4, 1979.

Penns Creek is a fertile stream, one of a handful that holds hatches almost every day of the season. Some writers call Henry's Fork in Idaho an "insect factory," where insects appear on the surface almost daily, and the chance to fish over trout rising to those insects is high. Penns Creek falls in the same category in the East. This limestone stream holds a wide array of hatches throughout the fishing season. In late March, for example, before many anglers think about fly fishing, Little Blue-winged Olives appear. The large down-wing Grannom caddis pops up in mid-April. This is followed by the Hendrickson and Quill Gordon into May, then the Gray Fox, Light Cahill, and Sulfur through June. The Blue-winged Olive, Yellow Drake, Slate Drake, Blue Quill, Trico and Caenis are midsummer's flies. The parade of hatches continues through October.

Most anglers associate Penns Creek with one hatch, however, the Green Drake.

The Green Drake and its Coffin Fly spinner cause quite a commotion on Penns around the Memorial Day holiday each year. Hundreds of anglers wrangle for a spot to fish, yet after the hatch has ended,

Penns Creek loses its appeal, as well as many of its anglers—despite the fact that other good hatches continue well after the Green Drake.

That particular Fourth of July morning began with light drizzle, overcast skies and cool temperatures—not great weather, but I have often had great fishing days in such weather. Three of us were on the stream that morning. At 9 a.m., the other two anglers had had enough of the weather, and were back in their car at the parking lot on Penns, their gear stowed.

I did just the opposite. I was just beginning. Bad weather or not, I was determined to get in a day of fishing. I decided to fish for an hour, see what happened, then go from there. I hiked the abandoned railroad bed upstream half an hour, to the lower end of Penns regulated water.

As I sat by the bank, taking in what was happening on the water, I noticed more than a dozen barn swallows flitting upstream, then downstream in a feeding frenzy. On the surface, a couple trout were also feeding on something.

I moved into the water and captured one of the thousands of Blue-winged Olive duns unable to escape from the water's surface. Evidently the hatch had just begun; otherwise those two anglers I saw in the parking lot would not have quit so early. Tying the Size 16 Blue-winged Olive Dun to my 5X tippet, I saw more trout rising—perhaps 30 trout were now feeding on dazed duns in front of me.

The first cast was a harbinger of the day ahead. The fly drifted only a foot before it disappeared. I set the hook and quickly netted a 12-inch streambed brown trout, released it, then hurriedly cast to another riser just upstream from me in a deep riffle. That fish also took the fly on the very first cast. I released that trout quickly, too, feeling like I had to hurry because I wasn't certain how long, under these conditions, the hatch would last. The drizzle might end, the sun peer through the clouds at any moment. I just didn't know. I'd seen cloudy skies clear and the hatch escape in normal rapid style—no more rising trout—before.

But that day, the trout gods were with me. Dark, cloudy skies continued for the entire Fourth of July and the hatch seemed to grow heavier as the day progressed. The trout seemed ravenous. They didn't quit for even a short break—a true feeding frenzy that lasted the entire day.

The Blue-Winged Olive Dun.

Very few trout in that first riffle refused my pattern, but after I caught and released about 20 fish, they quit rising. I noticed then that I had been fishing for two hours—and that I needed to change flies. The hackle, wings and part of the tail had almost totally disintegrated. But that was all right, because I had at least half a dozen other BWOs in Size 16 in my compartmented fly box.

A long deep pool lay ahead, where more than 30 trout were rising. Again, the fish were eager to rise to my fly...one, two, then three and four—I caught and released all of these trout as I moved up through the pool to the next riser. Would this never end, I wondered?

The second pattern became tattered, and I was thankful I had several more Size 16 BWOs in my fly box. Each time I tied a freshly groomed fly to my tippet, it grew shorter, but I didn't dare take time to restore it. I had no idea when this taste of fly fishing heaven would end, no idea when the weather, lousy for fireworks and barbecues, but great for catching Penns Creek trout on BWOs, might change.

A deep riffle at the head of the pool drew my attention. Here, a dozen or more trout fed freely in faster water. One fish appeared to be a hefty riser. On the first drift, a dark shadow slowly followed the pattern and refused it at the last second. The shadow couldn't resist the second drift, though. It slowly siphoned my BWO off the surface.

I set the hook, the line slashing water, and in a few moments, a stout 18-inch brown came to the net. That trout's belly was bulging from the BWO smorgasbord nature set before it. I could imagine hundreds of those olive-bodied mayflies in its stomach. Yet it continued to feed, to take advantage of a food surplus on an uncommon day.

Checking my watch, I saw that I had fished for more than five hours. Trout still rose upstream, and duns still rode the surface, but I decided I'd fished enough. I was tired. My arms ached from the thousands of casts I made that day, my legs were stiff from wading for five hours and the water wrinkled my hands.

Later, I estimated that I had caught in excess of 60 trout during that exciting and dramatic BWO hatch. I wished that I'd had someone along to share this with. And it turns out that I did, sort of:

I wrote about this one-of-a-kind event in *Pennsylvania Trout Streams and Their Hatches*. A month after the book came out in 1989, I received a letter from a reader, Andy Leitzinger, from Philadelphia, Pa. Turns out I wasn't alone. Two miles upstream Andy was also catching many Penns Creek trout on a Size 16 BWO during that cool, cloudy

July 4 hatch.

"I fished that day in complete solitude (I thought)." Andy wrote. "I was cold, happy and alone. I quit at 5 p.m. that day, my hands quite tattered from the teeth of many trout, because I had reached a state just short of exhaustion. I exalted the cold gray heavens above me and gave thanks for a wonderful and unique gift."

"I am glad to know that one other person was able to share the exhilaration I felt that day," Andy wrote. "Those days when everything comes together are few and far between and should never be taken for granted."

What a day! What a hatch! That Blue-winged Olive was by far the greatest hatch in intensity and length that I have ever witnessed in a lifetime of fly fishing. This was truly a remarkable experience, one that Andy and I will never forget—the hatch of a lifetime. And so far as we knew, we were the only two anglers who were there to appreciate it. I hope we all remember Andy's words, live by them and enjoy every fishing trip, savor the experience of each hatch. From best to worst, they really are all hatches of a lifetime.

Chapter 15
I Still Get Excited

"He stood at the edge of Cody's Rock and cast again, letting the fly rest upstream about midway in the current. I found myself thinking that each cast carried with it not only the hope of a trout on the rise, but a sense of renewal as well."

Harry Middleton
The Earth is Enough

I Still Get Excited

JOHN RANDOLPH, EDITOR OF *FLY FISHERMAN* MAGAZINE is a fantastic writer and fly fisher. We have fly fished many Pennsylvania waters together for more than two decades. I enjoy fishing with John because he's always asking questions, always learning. John's recent book, *Becoming a Fly Fisher*, is one of the finest to come out in the past 25 years. He has a way with words like no other fly fishing writer I know.

One chapter of John's book is called "Mentors." I have to chuckle when I read it, because John has me pegged when he describes how I react to a hatch; dashing to my car, grabbing a butterfly net out of the trunk, racing to catch one of the big white Green Drake Coffin Fly spinners we saw together.

Hatches, to me, are one of the most exciting aspects of fly fishing. I get seriously energized when a hatch occurs and trout are rising to the insects. I'm quite pleased when I've discovered a new hatch on a stream. Many people seem surprised I haven't lost my enthusiasm for fly fishing—especially when I encounter a hatch—since the very first hatch of insects that I matched on June 5, 1966. I've never lost that energy and excitement, and that first hatch-matching incident occurred more than 35 years ago.

Dallas, Pennsylvania was a great place to live back then. I moved there in 1965 as Director of Continuing Education for the Pennsylvania State University. I had fly fished half-heartedly for more than 20 years before I moved, but I'd often resort to worms and other tactics, especially when fly fishing was poor.

Tom Taylor and Lloyd Williams were my neighbors in Dallas. Tom fly fished frequently, and Lloyd had just started fly fishing again after a hiatus of more than a decade. Both continuously begged me to change my ways and to fly fish with them.

When the three of us finally agreed on a date to go fishing—June 5, 1965—I had the usual assortment of dry flies on hand, several Light Cahills, Adams, Royal Coachmans and a few Blue Quills, but little else.

Elk Creek, in north central Pennsylvania, was where we planned to fish. The stream was Lloyd's favorite in his younger years. He grew up in Canton, had a cabin on the upper end of Elk, and fished it for a half century, so he knew the stream well.

We arrived at the small stream at 5 p.m. and didn't do much for the first two hours. I kidded with Lloyd and Tom that I felt like using worms or a spinner and that if the fishing didn't get any better this would be my last fly-fishing trip. I learned later that Elk Creek was a fertile stream that held several quality hatches. The streams I had half-heartedly fly fished before had few if any hatches for me to match.

During our first two hours of fishing, not one trout rose. Then, in an instant, my whole life changed—forever. In the pool in front of me, a dense knot of light yellow mayflies appeared on the surface, and the trout—more trout than I could count—went crazy. A hatch was taking place, and during the hatch dozens of trout lost all their timidity. It was a feeding frenzy.

I was at the heavy riffle that entered the pool, while Tom and Lloyd fished below me—Tom at the tail out, Lloyd in the middle of the pool.

I captured one of the mayflies with my hat as it flew past me and examined it carefully. It was all creamish yellow—body, wings, tail and legs—and a Size 12 Light Cahill would definitely copy it accurately.

I yelled for Tom and Lloyd to tie on a Light Cahill, and within minutes all three of us drifted good imitations over rising trout on each and every cast. (It was something for Lloyd to fish a Light Cahill. Much of the summer his fly rod stayed in the back seat of his car with a Royal Coachman attached. He was always the first to cast a fly when we began fishing, because he never had to rig his fly rod.) With a few grumbling noises, Lloyd took off the Coachman and tied on a Cahill.

On my very first cast a trout sucked down that Size 12 pattern. I couldn't unhook that fish quickly enough. More fish rose in front of me and I wasn't certain how long this hatch would last. A couple more casts and another trout took the Cahill.

Craig Josephson shown here landing a trout on the Upper Verde River, still gets excited, too.

Meanwhile, just a few feet downstream, Lloyd and Tom had the same matching-the-hatch success. We all yelled and screamed like a bunch of kids at a carnival at each trout we brought in. Anyone who heard us would have thought we were three kids having a party. We caught more than 20 trout that evening during an hour-long hatch. And did I ever get excited at that initial matching-the-hatch episode.

That one exciting hatch started it all—my venture into fly fishing, not only as a hobby, but as a vocation. I became determined to fish the hatches in the future. To do that, I had to learn more about them, when and where they'd appear and how to match them. I'd read Schweibert's *Matching The Hatch* before, but I reread it several times that summer. I also read Art Flick's *Streamside Guide*, Leonard and Leonard's *Mayflies of Michigan* and Needham's *Biology of Mayflies*. I read everything I could on hatches and mayflies.

At the time, I couldn't have predicted I'd be writing about hatches in the future. But 12 years after that first incident that I wrote *Meeting and Fishing the Hatches*, designed to help other anglers easily predict and fish hatches. That day was the beginning.

I said earlier that I get especially excited when I feel I've discovered something new. Over the years I have found several great hatches that fueled my enthusiasm: Pine Creek, Pennsylvania's spectacular Brown Drake in 1972; the Trico hatch on the Verde River near Cottonwood, Arizona in mid-February; Tricos on the Salt River 15 miles outside of Phoenix on New Year's morning. No one had ever written about any of these hatches before.

The first time I saw a Trico hatch on Pennsylvania's Hoagland Branch, I got so excited that I just watched it, not fishing for half an hour. I was working on *Pennsylvania Trout Streams and Their Hatches* and planned to fish both Elk Creek and Hoagland Branch early one August evening. I wanted to write only about those streams I'd actually fished. I had a good idea what hatches these two small streams held, but wanted to fish both for a short while.

When I visit streams I often check spider webs for evidence of hatches. On the first bridge upstream on Hoagland Branch, I examined one of these webs and got a real jolt—Trico spinners still struggling to free themselves. I'd never seen a Trico hatch on a small mountain freestone stream before. Wow, what a first!

The lower end of this stream evidently held Tricos. But questions arose: How would I find out for certain that Tricos really existed here? How heavy was the hatch? Would trout rise for these diminutive mayflies? The only way to find out was to fish the stream in the morning. I forgot about my tight book research schedule—I had planned to fish several streams in the Tunkhannock area the next day—and decided to stay near the stream overnight and look for Tricos the next morning.

I don't camp. I hate it. After I got discharged from the Army in 1955, I swore I would never camp again. In my two-year tour of duty at Fort Bragg, North Carolina, our battalion camped out at least three evenings a week for two years—winter, summer, spring and fall. We camped in heat, cold, rain and snow…bleccch! True to my convictions, I have never camped since then, but stay in nearby motels, where I can find all the conveniences of civilization.

That evening, I traveled quite few miles to find a motel. It was dingy and old, but much better than a tent. I was excited about the next morning's prospects.

I was up early the next morning, eager to seek out what I might discover, and got back to Hoagland Branch about 7 a.m. At the bridge where I'd seen the Trico spinners the previous night, I searched the air above a riffle for Tricos. None visible, I walked downstream for a better view. There, in the middle of that small mountain stream with a heavy canopy, I saw thousands of glistening wings, Tricos mating, the final phase of their life cycle.

Excited? I was really bouncing that morning. I felt certain that no one had ever witnessed this hatch on this stream before. This was truly a first. But what good is a hatch to a fly fisher if no trout feed on it?

I walked downstream below the riffle, below a deep, 30-foot long pool. For a few minutes, nothing rose. Then one mountain brook trout, two and three began to feed on those small, spent spinners on the surface.

One thing still remained: I wanted to catch one of those risers on a Trico imitation. After watching for a time, I tied a Size 24 spent-winged Trico spinner on and cast upstream. That very first cast, one of the rising trout sipped in the copy.

I couldn't stop at just one so I fished a second riser. It also took the pattern—and so did the third one.

Yowza! Talk about getting excited! Not only did I see a previously unknown Trico hatch, but I caught trout rising to the spent spinner imitation.

I quit by 9 a.m. because I wanted to go downstream to Elk Creek and see if it had a Trico hatch. Hoagland Branch is an Elk tributary, so I figured there was a good chance for it.

I arrived at Elk a few minutes later and looked skyward. What I witnessed was an even heavier spinner flight than I had seen upstream on Hoagland Branch.

I was beside myself with excitement. I saw the Trico formation at the same place where I saw my first hatch 25 years before—the same pool where Tom Taylor, Lloyd Williams and I matched our first hatch and caught dozens of trout. I headed downstream along the banks of Elk to see if the hatch continued downstream. It did and I saw trout rising to it. In a way I felt like Christopher Columbus—I discovered Trico hatches on two small freestone streams that few if any other anglers knew about.

Another great discovery took place 40 miles west of Elk Creek and 20 years earlier, on Pine Creek.

I'd heard great things about this tremendously fertile trout stream. However, Pine Creek does have one tremendous problem: Water temperatures in the summer rise into the 70s and 80s and stay there for weeks. To cope, trout search for the cooler water in Slate Run, Cedar

Run and dozens of other cool tributaries and springs. (How I wish a bottom release dam were on Pine Creek at Blackwell. It would create a fantastic summer trout fishery.)

Jim Heltzel and I decided to fish Pine Creek—my second trip there—on the last day in May. Just two hours after we arrived, we were in the midst of one of the greatest, most dense mayfly spinner falls I have ever seen. The numbers of the spinners in the air were phenomenal. Many thousands of insects were moving upstream, just about 15 feet above the surface. Their wings in flight produced an eerie sound. And—I am genuinely not exaggerating—more than 100 trout rose to spent spinners in front of Jim and me.

I lost my excitement quickly, however, because I couldn't catch one of those darned trout. The spinner fall lasted for almost an hour and I finally managed to land one trout during that terribly frustrating evening. (Still, as many who have fished with me will tell you, I often get more excited about the hatch than I do catching trout.)

I captured a few of the mayfly spinners that evening and took them home for identification. Then I got really excited discovering that they were Brown Drake spinners. This also explained why I all but got skunked that evening... never having encountered that hatch before, I had no proper imitation. Actually, the Brown Drake in the eastern United States had never been mentioned before by other writers. (Acidic mine drainage from several mines upstream on Pine Creek has reduced the Brown Drake hatch. The Pine Creek Watershed Association is working to protect the river.)

The first time I encountered an Olive Sulfur hatch, I also made discoveries. For years I thought *needhami* duns were dark brown. Everybody who writes about them said they were. But the body of the female is really bright olive green. When I tied some female dun patterns with that olive green body, trout eagerly took that new fly.

I remember many exciting days over these many years. I'll never lose that exhilaration for hatches, the rise of emotion, the rising fish, having one trout after another take the imitation. If I ever do lose that edge, I'll wrap it up and call it a career.

Chapter 16

They're Trying to Kill Me

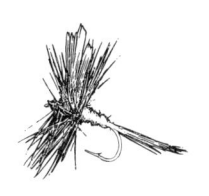

"I LAY UPON A FLAT ROCK where the water was four feet deep...."

THEODORE GORDON
American Trout Fishing

They're Trying To Kill Me...

I'VE FISHED MANY MEMORABLE WATERS IN MY LIFE. I've floated five rivers in Oregon, four in Washington, seven in Montana, and several in Wyoming, Colorado and Idaho. I've had my fill of great fishing on New Mexico and Arizona waters, and in the East. Yet I'd like to forget some of those trips.

Maybe it's me—it must be me—but I hate canoes with a passion. I find a lot of them unstable. I spilled several times and I swore I'd never enter another canoe.

But one day on the Clarion River, in northwestern Pennsylvania, Craig Josephson promised me that his canoe would be stable, that we'd have no trouble with the gentle flow. And I really had no choice in the matter if I wanted to float the Clarion so I could complete an article for the third edition of *Pennsylvania Trout Streams and Their Hatches*.

Craig got the aluminum canoe from Love's Canoe Rental in downtown Ridgway, and we boarded it, carrying our fishing gear and my camera with us. I was concerned about taking the camera, but Craig reassured me that it would be safe—we would be safe. We drifted slowly down this meandering river with very few rapids, and we fished as we floated.

It was late August, and several White Flies appeared early, but no trout fed. Suddenly I saw a trout rise and turned around to cast to it.

You know what happened next.... In a moment the canoe flipped and we went under—Craig, me, my gear, my fly rod, my $500 camera, everything. At the split second I hit the water, I was sure I was done for, then I surfaced, and began to assess the damage. Everything had water in it. Every fly box I had on that darned canoe had water in it. (Do you realize how long it takes water to enter everything you own when you capsize?) I grabbed some of my gear and swam to shore. Fly boxes gently floated downriver as we shook ourselves off. An instant of water destroyed my high-tech Pentax camera. No more photos that day.

That wasn't the only day I thought I'd drown. I was certain someone wanted me dead.

Mike Manfredo, Don Rodriguez and I planned to fish Phantom Canyon, on the North Fork of the Cache la Poudre River just outside of Fort Collins, Colorado. The Nature Conservancy—a fantastic organization that deserves a lot of credit for preserving many trout waters—maintains a beautiful stretch of the river there. (You'll see this small river and Don Rodriguez on the front cover *Fishing Small Streams with a Fly Rod.*)

Before we fished that morning, the Conservancy gave us a primer on snakes—dread of all dreads!—and the other dangers we might encounter on the float. They even gave us a whistle to put around our neck in case a snake attacked us or we fell and we couldn't get up. This should have been fair warning for me. I should have known they were serious.

A long, narrow, winding trail led down to the river. Workers cautioned us we might see poisonous snakes on the ledges along the trail. It took us more than half an hour to negotiate the trail before we ended up near the river.

A late August heavy Trico spinner fall was in progress. Trout rose in every visible pool and riffle. The three of us quickly headed for different river beats: I had the middle section, Mike was upriver and Don fished below me, about half a mile apart. I waded across the small river and out the other side. As soon as I reached the far bank, a six-foot snake greeted me.

Even though I was a biology teacher and had to handle them, I hate snakes, especially big snakes. I didn't care that it wasn't poisonous—it scared me. And that huge bull snake was downright rude. It reared its ugly head and hissed at me for more than a minute. It boldly stood its ground, not budging. I backed into the river and stayed there the rest of the day. No way was I walking the bank with huge snakes nearby. Any movement I made the rest of the day would be limited to the water.

Thank God I didn't have to move much that afternoon. After the Trico spinner fall ended, a Size 22 Blue-winged Olive hatch appeared and continued all afternoon. Trout fed in front of me for more than five hours. I stayed put. As far as I was concerned, the land belonged to the animals, especially the snakes.

Finally Mike called down to me and said it was time to head back up the trail.

If the snake didn't kill me maybe the hike up this steep hill would. It took me more than more than an hour to traverse the trail. Each step up that mountain I looked from side to side, leery of snakes hiding in crevices. Was I ever glad to get out of there.

I spent several winters in the Southwest before we officially bought our winter quarters there. I was officially designated as a snowbird—a resident of a cold weather climate who gets away for the winter to a warmer climate.

For me, that warmer climate was Arizona. Craig Josephson and I had spent several fishing trips in this Grand Canyon State and did quite well, and when Countryman Press asked me to write a trout fishing book on Arizona, I agreed. (Few people realize that arid Arizona has great fishing, more than 150 trout streams and rivers, plenty of wild rainbows, Apache and brown trout, and dozens of hatches.) In preparing for the Arizona book, I visited more than 40 rivers—many treacherous to reach and dangerous.

Fish the upper end of Tonto Creek near Payson, near the hatchery, and you'll see a small mountain stream with plenty of easy access. The same stream a mile below Kohl's Ranch is totally different. Here cliffs and steep gorges make the stream virtually inaccessible. The only way to fish some sections of this river is to swim from one pool to pool—I'm not kidding.

I remember fishing a section with Virgil Bradford one March day. We crawled over steep rocky cliffs in an attempt to reach the stream below. At one point I lost my grip and began sliding down the side of the mountain and into the water below. I got out of there quickly. I didn't want any more to do with that stream.

I've had other trips from hell—some I was certain that I wouldn't make it out alive. Fishing some of eastern Tennessee's waters haunts me still. One spring on the way home from Arizona, Jake Peppers of Townsend, Tennessee invited me to give a talk for their local fly fishing club, and fish for a couple of days in the Smoky Mountains. (I remember as a Penn State administrator the hostility of University of Tennessee football fans.)

After the talk Jake and two other friends took me to Abrams Creek for a day of early season fishing. They neglected some details about the trip—particularly getting into the stream. We hiked a narrow four-mile trail to reach our destination. On the way, they kept asking me if I was up to the hike. I wouldn't admit I was tired.

When we finally reached our goal, I wondered how we would get to the river. Peeking through an opening in the rhododendron, I saw a steep hill, and below it the river. For the first 200 feet, we crawled through a jungle of almost impenetrable vegetation. The last 100 feet I'd like to forget. I lost my grip on the hillside and slid abruptly into the deep chilly water for quite a splashy entrance. I was lucky I didn't break my fly rod.

For the next two hours of fishing, I didn't move. I couldn't—the water was too deep, too fast. I didn't catch any trout on that river—no one did. The whole exercise was futile. I was afraid for my life. Were these guys trying to kill me or what?

Then there was the return trip back to the car. I was barely able to climb back uphill to the trail, then had to hike four miles back to the car. Never, I vowed, would I participate in such a futile exercise again! I tried to forget this long ago. All anglers remember the rotten days in favor of kinder, gentler ones.

Almost a decade later, I gave a talk in Santa Fe, New Mexico. My host for the next two days was fly shop owner Manuel Monasterio. He asked me to give a couple of talks at his shop. As part of the tour, Manuel also scheduled a trip on the lower part of the Red River, 30 miles north of Taos, for Virgil Bradford, Ed Adams, himself and me.

From late December into early spring, huge hybrid cutthroat-rainbow trout (cutbows) move up the Red River from the Rio Grande below to prepare for mating. Ed guides on the river and is an expert fly fisher. Manuel is also an accomplished angler. He could easily be a guide.

Ed's first question on our river trip was if I was healthy enough for a hike down to the bottom of the canyon and back. "We don't want to be known as the anglers who killed Charlie Meck," Ed said.

The hike down the narrow, steep trail to the bottom of the canyon took an hour. Once there we spread out and each found beats in the river to fish.

It was a cold mid-December day. Huge cutbows had already paired up. It didn't take long to hook a trout. Manuel showed his expertise quickly and caught two heavy fish, and we saw a decent hatch of Little Blue-winged Olives, despite the cold. The pattern of the day was a Bead Head Glow Bug—all four of us were using this pattern by day's end.

Abrams Creek in Tennessee. We tried to enter the creek just below this area.

I hooked the last trout, but before it gave up, the big fish went downriver two, then three pools. Manuel went downriver after him and landed the lunker for me. What a way to end the trip...what a spectacular day! I enjoyed sharing it with these fishing friends. It was a shame we had only a few hours to fish this great river.

At 3 p.m., we had to head back up the narrow trail to the top of the mountain. I bent my head back and looked skyward. Manuel pointed to where the car was, where we had to go. Wow! Now I see why Ed Adams had asked what kind of shape I was in. Would I make it to the top? Even worse—would daylight run out before we arrived at the car?

While the other three anglers still talked at the river's edge, I started up the long, sky-high, narrow trail. I stopped on the way at least 10 times to rest for a bit and the other three passed me. Finally, as darkness covered the entire area, I made it to the top safely. Those last few steps, when I caught a glimpse of the car, as well as the beautiful New Mexico sunset, put a final bit of energy back in my legs. Tired, cold and no longer scared, I slept the entire hour trip back to Santa Fe.

Will they kill Charlie Meck? They keep trying, but they haven't succeeded yet.

◆   ◆   ◆   ◆

WHAT DO YOU TRY TO DO WITH LESS-THAN-SUCCESSFUL FISHING TRIPS, or embarrassing moments off the stream, when everything you try and do goes wrong? If you're like me, you try to forget them—wipe them out of your memory bank forever. Yet some disasters remain part of my psyche—and since I can't forget them, I'll write about them.

I can classify these unmemorable events in several categories: injuries to fellow anglers, falling in the water, being shut out or nearly so, and confrontations with anglers who had questions about one of my books.

When I first started writing for publication, I had no idea just how critical some readers can be—and how stubborn—and sometimes, how misguided. I met one of these readers face-to-face more than a decade ago, shortly after I'd finished my second book, *Pennsylvania Trout Streams and Their Hatches*.

I'd accepted an invitation from Barry Serviente to attend his first book fair in Carlisle, Pennsylvania. The fair featured some of the top fly-fishing writers in the nation, and created the opportunity for area readers to buy books and have them remarked. The fair opened at 10 a.m. I always get nervous when I am scheduled to autograph books. Several book signings were disasters, with few people to sign books for. On one occasion—supposed to be a two-hour signing session—I had three people buy books. Would this fair by Barry be such a disaster?

We didn't have to wait long to find out. By 9:30 a.m. more than 200 people waited in the halls just outside the room. Barry decided to open the session early. Wow! All those people and more showing up every minute, descended on the authors with their books. By 10:30 a.m. Barry sold out of my book. What was I to do now? I sat and chatted with people, and my wife listened to would-be buyers complain about not having enough books.

At 11 a.m., a man in his late 50s walked up to me and said: "There are no Light Cahills on Penns Creek." He repeated these eight words—with more emphasis. Then he yelled, "THERE ARE NO LIGHT CAHILLS ON PENNS CREEK."

I paid no attention to the rabble rouser and just kept talking to my wife. He yelled a fourth and fifth time. I was certain at this point that I had someone who was a bit mentally unbalanced. I tried to reason with him, but he didn't accept any explanation I gave. His voice became louder and louder until many of the people attending the book fair grew silent and stared in our direction. He wouldn't listen to a word I said.

Then this man opened his copy of *Pennsylvania Trout Streams and Their Hatches* and pointed to the hatch chart I listed for Penns. "Here, see this. You list Light Cahills on Penns Creek. Charlie Wetzel said there weren't any on that stream. You goofed."

He wouldn't leave. He kept shouting at me. I went over to Greg Hoover who was in the crowd and told him what the man was saying. Greg is a skilled entomologist who knows Penns Creek well. Greg agreed with me that this stream holds a good population of Light Cahills, but the man wouldn't listen. Finally, after 15 minutes of his yelling and harassing me, I walked away. I'd had enough. My poor wife had been sitting at the booth with me and when I left, he continued to yell at her for another 15 minutes. (Boy, did she give it to me when I came back to the booth.)

That's not the only time I got the devil for something I wrote. I write six articles a year for *Mid-Atlantic Fly Fishing Guide*. Recently, I wrote about a terrific hatch on Penns Creek, well after the hordes of Green Drake anglers had departed. This hatch often appears in late June and July. I encouraged anglers to look for and fish this hatch because they'd encounter few other anglers at that time of the year.

After the article was published, I received a letter from a Sunbury, Pennsylvania angler who was outraged that I'd write about a hatch he'd had all to himself. Evidently he had fished this hatch for years and encountered few other fly fishers. He was afraid I would create crowds in late season. He sent me a nasty letter and criticized me for sharing the hatch with others.

I've also had my share of embarrassing experiences on the water, one trip with Dave Engerbrettson—he passed away recently—to fish some productive lakes in central Washington in particular.

Dave was a popular writer and speaker on fly fishing. We fished one of the lakes at Isaak's Ranch one afternoon for some of its huge rainbows. Eight hours of fishing made us weary of casting. We were fishing a few yards apart, and before I knew what was happening, I heard Dave yelling, "Stop...stop, stop!"

I looked over at Dave and saw my tippet in his face, my big streamer fly in the lobe of his ear. I'd hooked the famous outdoor writer Dave Engerbrettson. Nice catch, but now what do we? We took Dave to a hospital for hook removal. On the way there, the hook came out on its own. How embarrassing....

Of course, accidents can happen, and even if I'm not the cause, if I'm the expert I feel responsible, as I did on a fishing excursion with Rick Wolfe, who worked for WPSX-TV at Penn State. For years I promised Rick I'd take him fly fishing. Finally, after a couple years of cajoling, we were headed for Bald Eagle Creek, near State College.

The water was high, so I handed Rick a Muddler Minnow and showed him the basics of casting. You probably know what happened next—on one of his very first casts, Rick hooked that Muddler through his own chin. I couldn't get it out so I decided to take him to the hospital emergency room. Rick called his wife from the hospital to tell her what happened. He never went fly fishing again.

In 1997, Craig Josephson set me up as a fishing guest on a weekly ESPN/Suzuki Outdoors program, focused on the streams and rivers near Spruce Creek, Pennsylvania. Craig felt it was a good way to generate publicity for my books. Larry Czonka, who did many hunting programs and some fishing programs, was the celebrity.

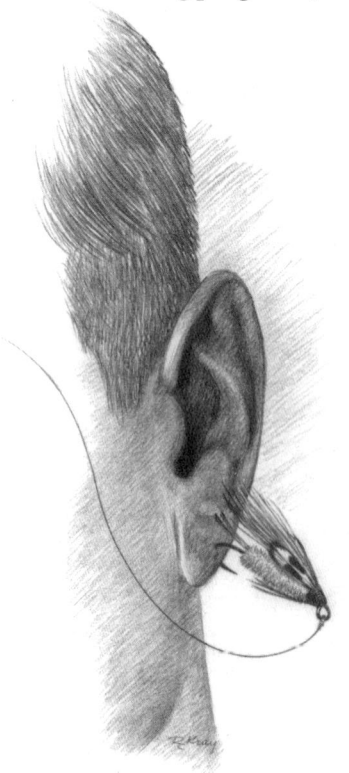

Craig set up overnight accommodations at quaint Arch Spring Bed & Breakfast, owned by David Morrow of State College.

Arch Spring consists of two pre-Revolutionary War era homes—one with a fort built in the backyard so colonial settlers could escape to it to fight Indians. Arch Spring also has the headwaters of one of the most unusual limestone streams I've ever seen, Sinking Creek. The creek begins as a spring, upstream from the house, then flows through an arched limestone rock passage underground, only to resurface 300 feet below the house before going underground again. I've never seen water temperatures rise above 60 degrees here. Even mid-July temperatures are 55-58 degrees. A stream-bred strain of brown trout and a good mid-May to mid-June Sulfur hatch inhabit the stretch, a quarter mile of great limestone fishing.

Part of the program was filmed on Sinking Creek during the peak of the creek's Sulfur hatch. Austin Morrow, a highly-skilled young fly angler, was our host for this part of the program. The cameraman filmed trout taking naturals and then taking my imitation. One evening when I matched the Sulfur hatch, I caught three large trout. Other days were spent fishing the Little Juniata River and Spruce Creek—where Larry and I managed a couple of 20-inch browns on the Six Springs section. Each day we caught plenty of trout and the video footage seemed to cover everything it should, including me tying flies, matching the hatch, and everyone catching plenty of trout. After four days of filming, we finished the videotape. This was late May. The producer said the final product would air in early November.

November, then December arrived; and I heard nothing about when the video would air on ESPN. Finally, Craig contacted the producer and they said that they had bad news for us: The video and the cameras got damaged because of water. I remembered that one day the cameraman fell in but I thought he'd saved the camera by holding it above the water.

I was embarrassed. We'd spent four full days on this project, convinced local private clubs to allow us to fish, got a bed and breakfast to give us free accommodations—and none of them got even a mention about anything. What a lousy deal…all the wasted time and energy that went into that project. I try hard to forget that fiasco.

There are other events I'd like to forget.

One evening I met Al Troth in Dillon, Montana to fish and talk with him about some of the local rivers. I had met Al years before on Penns

Creek in Pennsylvania. We both fished an exceptional Green Drake hatch that evening. He lived in central Pennsylvania for years before he moved to the West as a guide.

Al took me to the infamous Poindexter's Slough nearby, a fantastic but heavily-fished spring creek in southwestern Montana. Al didn't fish but told me where to fish and what to use. I fished halfheartedly that evening for two hours listening to Al and studying the stream and caught only two trout.

When I finished for the evening, Al pointed to the section I had just fished and boldly said: "I would have caught at least a dozen trout in that section you just fished." That's a statement designed to deflate your ego balloon.

These aren't all of the embarrassing monuments in my fly-fishing life. I have, thankfully, forgotten many. Try as I might, though, I can't forget these moments. They remain a part of my psyche.

Chapter 17
Great Rivers, Great Hatches, Great Guides And Great Memories

"LEARN TO IDENTIFY, AND TO FISH WITH, the "fly on the water." But do it for the plain, commonsense reason that you are thereby quadrupling your pleasure (to say nothing of rather more than doubling your bag)...."

J. W. DUNNE
Sunshine and the Dry Fly
(from *The Quotable Fisherman,*
by Nick Lyons)

Great Rivers, Great Hatches, Great Guides And Great Memories

AT A RECENT TALK, AN ANGLER ASKED ME WHICH BOOK was the most difficult, most challenging for me to write. Without hesitation, I told her the most complex book had to be *Great Rivers—Great Hatches*.

Deadlines, pressure and writing challenges—that book had them all. But completing the book also let me experience great rivers and great hatches, introduced me to great guides, and produced some fantastic memories.

Great Rivers began with a proposal to Stackpole Books. Greg Hoover (an extremely skilled Pennsylvania entomologist) and I would write a book detailing 62 of the top rivers across the United States. I chose Greg because of his hatch knowledge. The publisher agreed, but wanted the manuscript completed by September 1, 1991.

We wondered how we could cover everything—discuss each river, its characteristics and major hatches—effectively in just four months. Divide and conquer was the answer. I covered 43 of the rivers and Greg wrote about 19.

I agreed to cover the waters of Oregon, Washington, Idaho, Colorado, New Mexico, Wyoming, California, Utah, Montana, Pennsylvania, Virginia, Maryland, West Virginia and part of New York.

That meant a lot of traveling and fishing—14 states. In four months I had to travel, take photos, and successfully fish waters like Henry's Fork, the Madison River, Silver Creek, the Green River, the San Juan River, the Missouri River, the Bighorn River and dozens of other notable waters. It seemed like a Herculean task.

Maybe guides could help? But I had disdain for guides. What could they teach me? Besides, they're expensive to hire. I had never used a guide in my 30 years of fly fishing and thought didn't need one now. Mike Manfredo and I fished in New Zealand for a month and didn't use a guide. Why now?

Then I came to my senses: I had the deadline to meet. Who knows more about a river and its hatches than someone who fishes it on an almost daily basis? No way could I learn the hatches on each of these waters in the short time I had, so I hired a local expert or guide for each river. I didn't use a guide for many of the waters I frequently fished in Pennsylvania, New York, Maryland and Virginia, of course, but on most of the waters in the West I had a least one guide—in some cases several. Overall, I used 25 different guides.

Hiring those guides was one of the best decisions of my life, and it made that book possible. I saw some great hatches and some of the best fishing I'd ever seen. One guide taught me how to fish a tandem rig (two flies), another taught me proper high stick nymphing technique, a third showed me a great pattern, and on and on. More than 10 years later I still use a lot of what those guides taught me. I learned more than fishing from them, too. I was introduced to salsa on the trip down Oregon's Deschutes River. On Oregon's Williamson River we had a heater in the boat to combat the cold early spring chill.

The down side to the growing number of guides and guiding services on some rivers is ferocious competition—between guide services, and between anglers and guides. I've seen anglers and guides get into fights on New Mexico's San Juan River. More guides also means heavier fishing pressure and much more selective trout. I fished the Bitterroot River near Missoula, Montana in the mid-1970's, well before guides had appeared on this water. I had to walk into areas then, and I didn't see another angler in the entire week I fished. Returning to the same stretch in 1991, I saw guided McKenzie boats drifting past me the entire day.

In the 14 states and 43 rivers I fished to write the book, I saw a lifetime of hatches—50 in all. On waters like the Missouri, Kootenai and Henry's Fork I hit multiple hatch days. On Henry's Fork, my brother, Jerry Meck, and I saw Pale Morning Duns, Blue Quills and Blue-winged Olives. I hit one of the heaviest Little Blue-winged Olive and the greatest Pale Morning Dun hatches of my lifetime on the Kootenai just above Libby, Montana with Jerry and our guide David Blackburn. Jerry and I probably caught more than 50 trout that day thanks to the great Pale Morning Dun hatch and a great guide.

The Kootenai River and the Pale Morning Dun hatch.

A few weeks later, my son Bryan and I floated the Bighorn River in south central Montana with Richie Montella. That morning we drifted several miles downriver before Rickie pulled the boat to shore. As he did, Bryan and I saw maybe 20 trout feeding on a spinner fall. Richie told us to tie on a Pale Morning Spinner and we took turns casting to the pods of rising trout. Bryan and I caught 15 of those risers before the spinner fall ended.

The next day Bryan and I headed for the Missouri River in north central Montana. This adventure was unforgettable. We met our guides, Pat Elam and Mike Bay, in Craig, Montana for a day of float fishing. As we approached Craig about 8 a.m., I noticed a huge swirl between the road and the river. It almost looked like the huge dust devils so common in the West. As we got closer I saw what it was: a huge mating swarm of male and female Tricos, a swarm larger than any I had ever seen before.

Hundreds of trout, in a rhythmic process, slowly fed on spent spinners all over the river. These trout came to the surface, scooped in several spinners, then went beneath the surface a foot or two. They'd repeat this process every few seconds. Successful anglers tried to emulate this feeding rhythm. So many spent spinners fell that they almost covered the entire surface—a huge available food source.

One small Trico spinner imitation didn't stand a chance to catch a trout. Pat Elam handed both of us a Size 16 pattern that he called a Bouquet. It resembled three or four Tricos on the same hook. Finally,

I'll never forget that Pale Morning Spinner fall on the Bighorn River.

after a half hour of frustration, a trout hit the cluster and I landed my first Missouri River brown trout on a Trico spinner fall. Bryan and I landed only a few trout that morning—fishing that hatch and spinner fall can be extremely frustrating, often barren, because the spinners are so thick on the water the trout have too much choice.

Jay Kapolka accompanied me on the Oregon leg of the trip, a late May fishing marathon. I had already fished the western March Brown on the McKenzie and Willamette Rivers in April. With Jay I planned to fish the Metolius, Williamson and Deschutes Rivers.

We fished the Metolius River for an entire day, with little to show for our effort. It could have been the cold weather or maybe the time of year, but we did poorly.

The next day Jay and I fished the Deschutes with Craig Lacy as our guide. Two things stand out about that leg of the trip: a spectacular Salmon Fly hatch, and Craig helping me to refining my high stick nymphing technique. I enjoyed nymphing that day, especially witnessing all those salmon flies emerging from the river. Jay and I caught plenty of trout on a large black nymph that copied the Salmon Fly larva.

Our previous unsuccessful day on the Metolius still bothered me. The Metolius is generally considered a better river than the Deschutes, so we decided to give it a second chance. Central Oregon weather turned against us, but this actually improved the fishing.

A fine drizzle was falling when we arrived at the Metolius, and it was cold. Thousands of dazed duns were on the surface, with 30 trout busily scooping in as many as they could. The problem was the duns ranged from Size 12 to 18. Four hatches appeared simultaneously that afternoon, and for hours we fished over trout rising to each mostly olive hatch. What a day!

In early September, after Greg Hoover and I submitted the manuscript, I was ready for a break. I didn't fish for two weeks. The research for the book temporarily turned fishing into the drudgery I associated with deadlines. Small wonder, with all that fishing. After a break, I was ready to go at it again, though. However, the things I had experienced in those four months—some of the greatest rivers and hatches and guides will endure in my memory.

Chapter 18
Sink That Fly

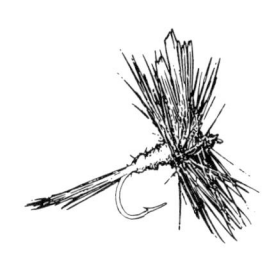

"Just as in cooking there's no such thing as a little garlic, in fishing there's no such thing as a little drag."

H. G. Tapply
The Sportsman's Notebook
(from *The Quotable Fisherman,*
by Nick Lyons)

Sink That Fly

MY EYESIGHT IS SLOWLY FAILING. The older I get, the more difficult it is for me to follow those small dry flies. I sometimes even have trouble following large dark flies like a Slate Drake or an Adams. Even though they are fairly large flies, they are often difficult to locate on the surface. I used to use Size 26, even Size 28 flies—but no more.

That's what frustrates me with the Trico hatch and spinner fall. These tiny mayflies appear in unbelievable numbers for three to four months a year. I don't care if you fish in the East, Midwest or the West, you'll see these critters on many trout waters in August, September and October, and in winter months in the Southwest.

A Size 24 often copies the Trico spinner, but with the heavy fishing pressure, people like Dick Henry have told me that they now rely on a smaller, Size 26 pattern. That's unthinkable for me—I just can't see the pattern well enough.

I take any advantage I can get—a strike indicator for instance—to help me locate dry flies. Sometimes, I fish smaller dry flies behind a larger one—if I can locate the larger one then I know approximately where the smaller one is. A few years ago I found a way to fish small spinner patterns and still see them easily, even with my poor eyesight.

An old man on Falling Springs Branch in south central Pennsylvania was part of an incident I've mentioned before, an event that occurred more than 25 years ago. I had an appointment on that late July morning at Penn State's Mont Alto Campus at 11 a.m. The campus is only three miles from the stream, too close not to fish almost every time I visited the campus. I purposely set the meeting that day for late morning so I could fish the Trico spinner fall before the meeting.

Under cloudy conditions that morning, the hatch and spinner fall lasted longer than usual. When I looked at my watch along the stream, it read 10:45 a.m. I had agreed to meet Clyde Johnson, Mont Alto's Director of Continuing Education, at 11 a.m.; I knew I was in trouble.

Add to this my frustration with the Trico hatch—I couldn't catch any trout on the spinner fall.

Falling Springs and many of the other Trico-holding streams get plenty of midsummer fishing pressure. On a good day, I might expect to land three trout. I would have settled for a single trout that morning—but I wasn't landing anything.

I saw an old-timer, a man about 75 years old, fish the spinner fall on the other side of the stream, 30 feet upstream from me. While I caught one (probably blind or retarded) trout, that old-timer landed half a dozen. And while I mumbled to myself, like Vince Marinaro did several years before, and changed from one pattern to next, this old angler kept catching and releasing trout.

I finally swallowed any pride I had left and walked upstream, directly across from that old angler and asked him what he was doing to catch all those trout. He wouldn't answer.

This has happened to me many times. It's probably happened to you, too. Ask me what I caught a fish on or what fly I'm having success with and I'll probably end up giving you one of the patterns—but many anglers seem to consider what their fly patterns as some sort of state secret or privileged information. It's frustrating, but I've found over the years that often-successful anglers won't give you a direct answer.

Neither did this secretive old codger. He just looked at me, paid no attention to my question, and continued to fish. Ten minutes later, he wound up his line, turned around and headed for his car, parked just a hundred feet away.

Just as he turned he muttered four words that I still remember as well today as the day I heard them: "I'm sinking the fly." He said nothing else and continued towards his car.

What did he mean? I pondered that answer on my hurried trip to the Mont Alto Campus—I was late—and during the meeting at the campus and well into the afternoon.

I went home that evening, sat at my fly tying desk and began tying. That old timer said to sink the fly so I tied a dozen weighted Trico patterns. I used hen fibers for the tail, opossum fur for the body and Flashabou for the wings. Before I tied in these materials I wound five wraps of .005 lead wire around the shank of the Size 24 hook. I placed these sunken spinners in a separate compartment next to my regular Trico patterns and there they stayed for more than a decade. I almost forgot about those spent-winged spinners completely. But in 1998 on the Ruby River, I got a chance to use those sunken spinner patterns.

Jake and Donna McDonald operate the Upper Canyon Ranch—focused at anglers, hunters and other vacationers looking for a place to enjoy the outdoors—just south of Alder, Montana. It is a small outfit as Big Sky ranches go, yet the ranch forms part of the southern boundary for one of Ted Turner's ranch properties. Anglers know Alder for several things: One is two noted town residents, Stinky and Pugh. Another is the town's steak house, a great place to eat. I always leave their place weighing more than I did when I came because the food is so good.

After our previous—and to me infamous—Ruby River horseback trip, Jake and Donna got the idea for a fly fishing workshop at their ranch. They had a classroom building and wanted to use it for fly fishing workshops during the next fishing season.

Jerry Armstrong was Jake and Donna's resident fly fishing guide. Jerry's home is in Chambersburg, conveniently near Falling Springs, which gave Jerry and me a chance, that winter, to outline and plan the Upper Canyon Ranch workshop program for the following August.

August's fly fishing workshop had ten people registered. I came a day early to get to know the river a bit better. We planned to fish the Trico hatch, then have classes after lunch and fish again in the evening. I wanted to see—and fish—the Trico hatch on the river before I had students to deal with.

I was on the river at 8 a.m. that morning. Clouds of spinners already covered some of the faster sections of the water, and a light breeze blew some of these into my face. By 9 a.m. thousands of spinners fell onto the surface and a few trout began rising. I cast, cast, cast, but not one of the few trout rising took my spent spinner pattern.

By 10 a.m., I had company—several of the workshop registrants had arrived, also a day early. They heard at the ranch that the instructor for the week was fishing the river, and came to see how well I fished the spinner fall.

It's bad enough to get frustrated when you can't catch any trout and you're by yourself, but much, much worse when you have an audience, especially tomorrow's students! Would they believe anything I said if I couldn't catch any trout during a prolific spinner fall?

I mentally replayed my choices for that day's fishing, trying to come up with something that would achieve some success. What can I use to catch these trout? I would have tried anything—short of live bait—because I was desperate, worried that the workshop the following day would be a failure.

Finally, inspiration struck. I remembered those weighted Tricos I'd tied more than a decade earlier. I opened my fly box, grabbed one of the weighted spinner patterns and tied it to my 6X tippet. Would it work?

More than half the workshop students had been watching me get more frustrated as the spinner fall went on. They watched as I tied the weighted Trico spinner behind a Size 18 Patriot dry fly, a spinner pattern that copied many of the naturals falling onto the surface upriver. By the time those spinners reached the pool I was fishing, carried on the current, they had sunk beneath the surface. I used a two-foot tippet, connected it to the bend of the Patriot dry fly with an improved clinch knot, and tied the weighted spinner on the end. The spinner pattern would sink and the small dry fly would act as a strike indicator. I clumsily and hurriedly cast that fly combo upriver into the riffle at the head of the pool. I knew the spinner fall would soon end and I didn't have much time to redeem myself.

On the third cast, the Patriot dry fly sank beneath the surface and I set the hook. Wonder of all wonders, I brought in a 12-inch rainbow.

Now the students watching from the far side began mumbling. Maybe they were saying, "It's about time." I know I looked skyward and thanked God that I hadn't made a fool of myself.

Within minutes another trout hit that sunken pattern, then another and another. By the time I released the fifth trout the group began applauding. Wow! That weighted imitation turned a potential disaster into a success. Maybe they'd listen to what their teacher says tomorrow. That sunken spinner pattern saved the day for me then and has repeated this success several times.

Bob Budd, a good friend and a fantastic fly fisher, rarely gets a chance to fish because his three kids demand a lot of his time. Just a week after the episode on the Ruby River, Bob found a couple of hours for Spring Creek in central Pennsylvania. I asked Bob to try the sunken spinner pattern and told him the success I'd had just the previous week in Montana. During the spinner fall that morning, Bob picked up a half dozen trout.

So next time you get frustrated with a hatch or a spinner fall—maybe the insect is too small for you to see or you think you've matched the hatch but nothing works—try a new tactic. Listen to that old man's words: "Sink that pattern."

Chapter 19

Okay, Now Catch A Trout

"If a new man is particularly attentive he can learn to fly fish in half an hour. But then he will go on learning as long as he fishes for trout."

Arthur R. Macdougall
The Trout Fisherman's Beside Book
(from *The Quotable Fisherman,*
by Nick Lyons)

Okay, Now Catch A Trout

WHEN YOU'RE THE EXPERT, YOU CAN BE PUT ON THE SPOT pretty easily, both when you're fishing and when you're lecturing about fishing. I can remember at least two occasions when, after I gave a presentation, the group asked me to go over to the stream and catch a trout on command.

This is difficult—especially when you have an audience. You're putting your reputation on the line should you accept these challenges, and no disclaimer you can make about "not being the fish's boss" will mean a thing to that group.

One of these "catch on command" presentations was in Nemacolin, in southwestern Pennsylvania. Every year near the first day of fall, a group of Pittsburgh notables gathered for a weekend of fishing and fun south of Uniontown on Beaver Creek. For 20 years, this event (discontinued now) was known as "The Encampment." Darryl Bassett, assistant director of The Encampment, can vouch that The Encampment usually had about 200 people.

My program, attended by about 30 anglers, was called "How to Catch More Trout." As soon as I finished the presentation, one of the class members raised his hand and said, "Okay, now go over to the stream and catch a trout." Evidently all guest speakers for the past four years were asked to do the same thing. They'd asked Gary Borger to do it the year before.

I was in a bind. I couldn't very well say no. I had no valid excuse that I could escape on, no valid reason to refuse. I had a fly rod I used to demonstrate to the group and the stream was just 100 feet away. Two flies were already connected to the leader, so I was ready to fish. Not until I walked over to the stream did two group members tell me how lousy fishing had been that weekend.

"Two trout is all we caught so far today," someone said, upon our approach at a still, deep pool. Uh-oh…30 people, and they caught only two trout that morning. My success didn't seem likely.

It was a fairly warm day, but trout had been stocked for the event, so the water held plenty of fish. I looked skyward and prayed that I not make a fool of myself.

I had tied the tandem for the group and showed them how to use it, but I had just learned the tandem that year and brought it back with me from my recent western trip. Since there was no hatch that afternoon, I tied on a tandem made up of a Patriot dry fly and the infamous Green Weenie as the wet fly. If anything would work on these brookies the Green Weenie should.

On the very first cast in that deep pool I saw a large brook trout come off the bottom, slowly drift with the Green Weenie and finally take it. Wow!

I landed the heavy brook trout in front of the group and walked away. I didn't want to take a second chance—I knew I'd been lucky. I could have fished for several more hours and not caught another trout. As I backed away from the bank after I released the fish I said, "Now that's how it's done."

The group looked on in awe and spontaneously applauded. They didn't realize how lucky I'd been to have any fish take the fly at all. In fact, I'm certain I caught that trout only because it had never seen that ugly Green Weenie pattern before.

The Yellow Breeches Anglers Club holds an annual outing at the Allenberry Resort in Boiling Springs, Pennsylvania early each April. Several years ago they invited me to be one of their guest speakers. At that talk, I showed them four ways to catch more trout. Of course, the inevitable happened. Someone suggested that I go down to the stream and catch a trout with the methods I'd just discussed.

This would have been fine under normal conditions, but that day wasn't normal. The stream was a foot above normal and cloudy—extremely poor fishing. Catching a trout would require a miracle.

I tried to back out of it, but the audience pushed until I had no choice. Failure—making a fool of myself—seemed certain. I was sure I would embarrass myself in front of the 20 anglers who followed me to the stream.

Getting ready, I remembered an incident on Yellow Breeches three years before, when I fished this same stretch of water. For two days, the water ran high and off-color. The first day, Craig Josephson and I had fished high, cloudy water and never caught a trout. When we quit for the evening, we talked to another angler at the bar and told him our sob story about not catching trout, not even having a strike. This guy smiled, then claimed he'd caught 20 trout that evening. A few drinks later, we found out he was a used car salesman. Suddenly his story was full of little old ladies only catching trout on Sundays.

Back to the stream...I was setting myself up for a big fall, downplaying my skills in the event I did fail, and making the standard "I can't boss the fish," and "Consider the conditions," qualifiers.

Wading into the water, I wondered what would happen. I was fishing another tandem rig, a Patriot and a Bead Head Pheasant Tail, and began casting. As I described what I was doing, the dry fly sank into that high muddy water, and I set the hook. Wonders of wonders—a trout had hit the Pheasant Tail pattern, probably by mistake—and I caught it. Again I quickly and triumphantly waded out of the water and said to the group, "Now that's how it's done."

No way did I want to test my luck again...someone was watching out for me.

One more...this one involved a video director.

In 1992, Craig Shuman of Seattle, Washington wanted to do a video on fishing the Yakima River. Craig contacted Al Novotny of Casper, Wyoming to put the video together. He is truly a great producer, having done dozens of travel videos for Kodak in a travelogue series, some taking top honors. The Travel Channel also shows his videos from time to time. The Yakima video, entitled "Guide to Washington's Kittitas and Yakima Valleys," would be one of his first fishing efforts, however. And as the video's guest fly fishing experts, Dave Engerbrettson and I were under the gun—we'd have to catch trout or else Al had no video.

Dave was a well-known writer and fly fisher from eastern Washington. (He passed away recently.) He taught fly fishing at Washington State University, did a fly tying program for the Public Broadcasting System and wrote frequently for *Fly Fisherman* magazine. He was also an expert caster. But at that time, Dave's eyesight had suffered because of his diabetes.

Craig Shuman, a consummate organizer, set up the entire program for the week. (If you want something done right, have Craig do it. He is a perfectionist.) To get a 50-minute videotape, the group planned to float the Yakima for an entire week. Craig coordinated with manufacturers for fishing gear, shirts and jackets, and we all looked like models wearing the same blue neoprene waders and blue fishing vests.

The first day Al Novotny devoted to hardware fishing. Al felt obligated to take some video of spinner fishing because one of video's sponsors was a spinner manufacturer. It was a horrible day. In the entire five-mile float down the Yakima, the hardware guest angler caught just one trout. Al shot video of that fish out of the water and in the water for more than five minutes. He had to get all the footage he could.

We arrived at the river early for our part of the shoot. Dave and I were in one boat, while Al, his wife Carol, and son Jared, floated in the second boat with the video equipment. For the next four days Dave and I were under the gun. We had to catch some trout. Al wanted plenty of trout footage, and we were in luck from at least one standpoint—the Mother's Day hatch was on. Anglers call the hatch by that name because this small down-wing caddis fly appears around Mother's Day weekend in mid-May.

Thousands of those black caddis flies filled the air along the far bank as we entered the two McKenzie boats. Trout dimpled the surface everywhere as Dave and I readied our gear. Maybe we'd be lucky in matching the hatch and catching fish with our imitations, but I was nervous. I just hoped I didn't make a fool of myself.

Dave and I tied on Size16 Black Caddis down-wings and began casting. As soon as we began our casts, Al pointed the video camera at us and shouted, in all seriousness, "Okay, now catch a trout!" He was dead serious. The producer had given an order, and we were supposed to obey. I guess Al didn't realize that he should have given that order to the trout, not to us. Dave looked at me and I at him and we began to laugh. "Okay, catch a trout" became the catch phrase of the week.

We didn't comply with the director's order immediately, but half an hour later, I managed to obey his command. I hooked a 15-inch rainbow. Al took plenty of video. I wondered if he thought it would be the only one we caught that day. For a moment, it felt like the pressure was finally off my back. Surely, we could relax a bit, now, I thought. But the moment I released that trout, a second order barked across the water. "Now, catch another trout." It seemed to echo across the river from bank to bank.

Dave caught the next one and that eased the pressure for a few more minutes, but the producer demanded another, and another, and another trout. The caddis fly hatch that week saved the video. Al took plenty of video of the caddis, the pattern and trout we caught. Our producer's urgent demand had been answered—but he seemed insatiable in his need for more trout. Al always wanted just one more trout—maybe one a bit larger—to get that final shot for the video. Did he ever learn that you can't always boss the fish around? Not when we caught fish when he told us to!

"Okay, now catch a trout," still rings in my ears when I fish, especially when I think about those four days on the Yakima River.

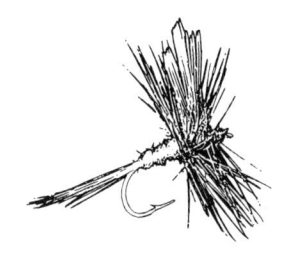

Chapter 20
The Case For Catch-And-Release

"THE ANGLER DOES NOT NEED DEAD TROUT in his basket to feel satisfaction. He has long since proved to himself that he can catch trout, and needs no proof for his companions."

ERNEST G. SCHWIEBET, JR.

The Case For Catch-And-Release

I WAS A LATE BLOOMER. I didn't get behind the wheel of a car until months after I had celebrated my 18th birthday. I didn't go to college until I was 25 years old—for the first two years after high school graduation, I worked as a "pants stretcher" at Boltz Knitting Mills in Pottsville, Pennsylvania. (Try explaining that job title to teenage friends.) If you wanted to find me after I finally passed my driver's exam, you'd look for me at work or on a nearby stream, Bear Creek in southern Schuylkill County, Pennsylvania. Immediately after work I'd head out to the creek to fish for a couple of hours. I killed every trout I caught for a few years, though my mother didn't want to cook them. Each spring my mother would clean out last year's catch from our small freezer at home and toss them in the trash. What a waste! I finally got the message and began returning the trout I caught.

One day on Bear Creek, I hiked half a mile upstream from the bridge I usually fished to a new section of the creek. There I'd discovered that someone had built a small dam on the stream. I wanted to see if this section held any trout.

Although it occurred more than four decades ago, I vividly remember the Yellow Sally wet fly I used. I saw lots of insects in the air and some fish rising to them—this was long before I knew anything about the hatches—I tied on a Yellow Sally because that pattern had the same general coloration as the bug in the air.

Fish surfaced all over that deep pool, and to my delight, I had made the correct choice. Thirty trout took my fly that evening. I think I caught half a dozen trout on the first 20 casts.

It was unusual that someone had evidently piled up rocks and deepened the pool by a foot or more. Where had all of these trout come from? The stretch had never been stocked before. Did the state plant the fish? Did the landowner do it? The water was not private.

I didn't know the answer, but I fished that same area each evening for the next two weeks. I told no one about this honey hole. I kept the secret spot to myself. Not even my best angling friends knew about the hot spot. I wanted this great fishing to last for the entire fishing season if possible; I wanted it to be my own private trout fishing club, a paradise with plenty of trout and no fishing pressure. If I continued to return these trout I could fish over them all season long.

I promised myself the pleasure of returning the next day, again by myself. The next trip didn't fail me; I caught a couple dozen trout. On each evening during those first two weeks I caught plenty of trout; some the same trout I'd caught before.

You know what happened, of course. Somehow, some way, someone else discovered my paradise. Maybe the deputy who had surreptitiously planted the trout told the intruder. It doesn't really matter. Another angler got wind of it, and started showing up every evening. He did a number on those beautiful fish. All the trout I had returned the past two weeks now became fair game to this uninvited member of my self-proclaimed private club.

Boy did I get upset when this angler approached me one evening, opened his creel and displayed eight huge brook trout—all dead. No longer would they hit my fly. He carried them in a heavy, wet, bulging canvas creel. The creel strap reddened the angler's neck from the weight of all of the fish in it. And for the next four evenings I met the same angler at my pool, his canvas creel heavy with dead fish.

Fishing success in that area declined precipitously. Where I averaged 20 to 30 trout per day for the past two weeks, catching six trout in an evening was considered lucky. Soon, six became two, and I no longer returned. Trout paradise was suddenly barren water. I had probably caught and released many of those fish, but now they were gone forever.

This disturbing event was the beginning of my decision, and recognition of my critical need—to return trout.

Another incident solidified the absolute need for catch and release in my mind.

In 1972, when I moved from Wilkes-Barre to State College, the late Mark Davis wanted to show me some new water on the nearby Little Juniata River. The river, although never stocked with hatchery fish, teemed with huge trout. Earlier that year, Hurricane Agnes, which dumped more than 12 inches of rain on the watershed, had flooded the entire region. Joe McMullen's Spruce Creek trout hatchery on a tributary of the Little Juniata was decimated, and hundreds of trout, some up to 20 inches long, escaped from his hatchery and made the half-mile journey downstream into the Little Juniata.

Mark and I arrived on the river in mid-July; about two weeks after the flooding had subsided. The area looked like a disaster zone, with huge trees strewn throughout the valley. After the initial shock of seeing this, Mark and I focused on fishing.

Light Cahills filled the early evening air, and trout all over the river began rising. More than thirty trout took our Cahill dry flies that evening. It was fantastic—I would return the next evening.

The next evening I did return, with another friend. I asked him when we arrived to promise that he would not kill any trout and he consented. We experienced the same success and released nearly 30 trout, all over 12 inches long. My fellow angler was excited about the river and its hatches and came back the next evening with an angler friend of his.

The third evening, I arrived at the same stretch and headed downriver to the area I had fished the previous two nights.

What I saw made me sick: Howard, the friend I had brought to the river the evening before, was heading out of the river with a friend. Both had huge willow creels filled with precious trout from the river. Howard's friend opened his creel, proudly displaying his catch. They were all 12- to 20-inch brown trout. Howard didn't show me his trout—he knew I was angry and upset that he'd not only broken his word, but had shared information given in confidence with another angler. I didn't say a word to either one, but they knew.

You know what happened to the river and that huge trout population. Word got around and more and more anglers fished the water, killing more and more trout. By July of the next year the trout population had been decimated. The river reverted to its former barrenness.

When will anglers learn? If we want to catch more trout, we've got to release trout. (I know I'm preaching to the choir.) The quality of the Little Juniata's fishery went downhill until the state Fish and Boat Commission began to plant fingerlings. In recent years, the river's new regulations returned it to one of the top waters in the East, but consideration of the resource by anglers would have meant that the stream's trout population wouldn't need to be renewed—it would have been a self-sustaining ecosystem.

Even some anglers who release trout can cause significant harm and probably kill more trout than they should. What upsets me more than anything is an angler who continuously holds a trout out of the water while a friend takes photos. When I see that on television, I yell for the angler to return the trout. I hate seeing anglers playing a fish in warm weather or when the streams temperatures are high. If I fish on extremely warm days in July or August and I don't want to harm the trout, I use a tandem rig made up of a dry fly and a wet fly. The dry fly acts as a strike indicator. I've used this rig for almost a decade now. On a warm day I often don't set the hook. On one occasion on a hot late July afternoon that dry fly sank more than 20 times. Even though I didn't set the hook two of those fish hooked themselves.

I've seen would-be do-gooders return trout they overplayed to the river—and watched the fish float by, belly up. They never recovered. I hate to kill trout, and to see trout killed. Anyone who fishes with me must agree to that premise. To this day I know some highly-skilled fly anglers who kill their limit almost every time they fish. It's the "you or me" attitude: If I don't kill them, somebody else will. Another excuse they use is that they only kill stocked trout or maybe only rainbow trout because they don't belong in a stream. No excuse is valid to me. If we want to enjoy the sport more, we've got to return the fish to where they belong.

How do the professionals working with trout feel about returning trout?

"We're different from hunters," said Tom Greene of the Pennsylvania Fish and Boat Commission several years ago; "we have the opportunity to release our quarry." Greene strongly believes in selective harvest. A small harvest on a dense population of trout won't hurt, he said, but coldwater fisheries that hold a sparse number of trout could definitely benefit from a catch and release program. Taking fish out of a low-population area causes further stress on an already over-stressed resource.

Look at the benefits of catch and release:

• SOMEONE ELSE CAN ENJOY CATCHING THAT SAME TROUT on another day. During a summer I spent on Bowman Creek, just north of Wilkes-Barre, I caught—and released—the same brook trout on five separate occasions. How do I know it was the same trout? It had an unusual marking on one side and a damaged eye. That same summer I talked to several others fly fishers who swore they'd caught that same trout.

Ask Paul Weamer of the Ultimate Flyfishers.com in Hancock, New York how many times he caught the same trout on one central Pennsylvania stream. He'll tell you about the same rainbow with easy-to-identify features that he caught four times in one season on the same stretch of water.

- RELEASING TROUT IN STREAMS THAT RECEIVE NO STOCKED TROUT is especially important. Waters that receive no hatchery trout take a long time to replace stream-bred trout. How long? Several years. On streams that depend on natural reproduction it's imperative to return most trout. An article I wrote about a stream that held a good number of stream-bred brown trout resulted in some notoriety for that stretch of water. After the article, I noticed the water got a huge increase in angling pressure, and more trout were killed, resulting in fewer hook-ups. That stream had never seen a planted brown trout. Sure, some of its tributaries were stocked—how it received its original supply—but the stream-bred trout that result from that are a valuable resource. Killing fish reduced that resource for everyone.

- A RELEASED TROUT will sometimes take a fly within a few minutes after you free it: On central Pennsylvania's lower Bald Eagle Creek, I hit the height of the Sulfur hatch in mid-May. A bulky trout fed directly across from me, just behind a log. I cast my Sulfur imitation about two feet upstream from the riser and he took the fly. I set the hook, but the trout didn't budge. Within a minute the hefty brown trout came completely out of the water, breaking the 5X tippet. Quickly, I tied on new tippet and another Sulfur and began looking for new risers. From behind the same log, another heavy trout was taking Sulfur duns. Again, I cast upstream, and after it floated a foot, a trout slurped in the fly. When I was releasing the fish, I removed two Sulfurs from the trout's mouth, the fly attached to my tippet, and the fly I'd just lost. The same thing happened during a horrendous day on Snake Creek in northeastern Pennsylvania. That day, I waded above my hip boots, missed a ferrule connecting my gear, and when I finally hooked a heavy rainbow on a Patriot dry, it jumped and broke the fly off. I fished upstream for another half an hour, had enough, then headed back down for the car. But I couldn't pass up a cast to that same riffle where I'd just lost the trout. You know the story. The first cast hooked a fish, and when I opened the rainbow's mouth, it had two Patriots in its jaw. Maybe it wasn't such a bad day after all.

• COMPARE A CATCH-AND-RELEASE SECTION OF A STREAM with an area of the same stream without such regulations. A good example is Caldwell Creek in northwestern Pennsylvania. I fished the stream one late April afternoon with local fly fishing expert, Jack Busch. Jack and I hit one of the best combinations of early season hatches we could expect to see; first the Hendrickson, followed in quick succession by a Blue Quill. Jack and I fished in open regulations water (catch and kill) for the first hour of the hatch and saw only two trout rising. Trout remains were scattered all about the stream bank, however. When we moved upstream to the catch and release area on the West Branch, we saw dozens of rising trout and caught many fish.

• RELEASING TROUT OFFERS ANGLERS A SENSE OF SATISFACTION. For years my son, Bryan kept many of the fish he caught. A year after he took up fly fishing exclusively, he caught a 20-inch holdover brown on the Little Bald Eagle near Tyrone. I still remember him looking up at me as he stooped over to release that fish. He smiled and said that he hoped he could catch the same trout another day. I knew at that moment that he had matured as a fly fisher.

It's been more than 20 years since I killed my last trout. I even release trout on marginal water. Why, I don't know; even though I'm convinced that most of the trout on warmer waters will die. This past June, I caught several trout on a section of Bald Eagle Creek where dozens of browns were stacked up just below a cool tributary entering the main stem. Even though I knew these trout had little chance to survive the summer water temperatures, I released them. It was just the right thing to do.

Jim Misuira told me of an incident about a Lackawanna River angler who killed some of the larger trout on that recovering river, took them home and used them as fertilizer for his garden. Jim knows this person. What a colossal waste! Remember that the next time you're tempted to kill a trout.

Anglers have a momentous choice: Release trout to catch another day and make another angler a little more satisfied, or kill them. The best anglers leave the environment we enjoy the way we find it—and this means returning trout. What was once a shallow phrase to me has now become a crusade. Return your catch.

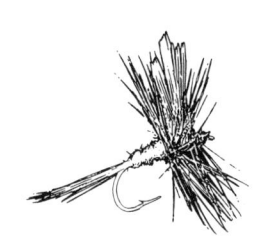

Chapter 21
My Secret Stream

"THE STREAM IS A BOOK with an endless number of pages; no matter how well one reads or how long, he will always be coming on new and exciting chapters."

CHARLES E. BROOKS
*Nymph Fishing for
Larger Trout*

My Secret Stream

SECRET STREAMS HAUNT MY FISHING MEMORIES. I fished my first secret stream—or at least a section of a stream—more than 50 years ago, that Yellow Sally stretch of Bear Creek that someone had secretly dammed and stocked. I considered it my private trout paradise—until another angler stepped in. My first secret stream was lost to the greed of a kill-trout angler, but it wasn't the only special honey hole I've discovered and treasured.

About 10 years ago, I discovered another secret water teeming with wild brown trout and great hatches. Whispers suggested this stream held great numbers of huge brown trout and some good hatches. Friends had fished this same water for the past 15 years and caught some brown trout well over 20 inches long. They talked in low voices about browns rising to tremendous Sulfur, Light Cahill, White Fly and Green Caddis hatches. Now the time had come to find out if the reports were true.

Harry Redline, a retired waterways patrolman and an excellent fly fisher, first showed me the stream. Our first trip coincided with the height of the Sulfur hatch. By the time we reached our fishing spot, dozens of Sulfur duns had already emerged in the fast water above, and several big trout were executing straggler duns and emergers from feeding positions in a heavy riffle.

I couldn't wait—I began casting as soon as I connected the Sulfur dry with a clinch knot to my tippet. That first cast was over a lunker. It hit and ran me down into my backing. Wow! I finally landed the brown—it looked about 18 inches long—used a hemostat to remove the fly deep in its mouth and quickly released it.

I was in a hurry to cast over the next surfacing trout. The next closest riser inhaled the dry fly and again took me into my backing.

I didn't want the hatch or the evening to end. It did, however, but not before I landed more than 10 trout that averaged 16-18 inches long. Most risers took the artificial on the first drift. All these huge wild brown trout, the great hatch…what an experience!

One lesson I've learned fishing this and other relatively low pressure waters over the years is that I can usually tell how heavily fished a stream is by how selective the trout are. If trout continuously take the pattern on the first drift, the water receives little pressure. If it takes four or five perfect drifts over a riser to have him take an artificial, the stream gets heavily fished.

Fish Tulpehocken Creek near Reading, Pennsylvania, or the South Platte below Elevenmile Reservoir in Colorado just once and you'll see what I mean. Tony Gehman and Dave Eshenower of Tulpehocken Creek Outfitters and I know how it is almost impossible to hook a trout on that creek some days. We fished together there a few years ago, and the Tulpehocken's trout strike—and let go—the instant they feel an artificial, especially if they've been hooked before.

Phil Camera and I shared a fantastic Trico spinner fall on the fertile South Platte just below Elevenmile Reservoir one morning. Huge trout fed within feet of us, seemingly undisturbed. We figured the trout saw so many anglers, they'd grown accustomed to them.

On my secret stream, the huge brown trout are not nearly as selective.

Paul Weamer, a young, highly-talented fly fisher and a great fly tier, has a tremendous head start on the sport. He ties hundreds of dozens of flies annually for Mary Dette, and manages a fly shop in Hancock, New York on the Delaware River.

For years Paul also *had* his own secret stream. (Note the italics.)

For years Paul fished a stream near his central Pennsylvania home in Ashville. The stream held some good hatches and a great population of wild brown trout. The stream had recently rebounded from a severe bout with acid mine drainage. Paul caught some big trout there. For five years he saw few other anglers fishing the stream. The Pennsylvania Fish and Boat Commission found out about the stream, conducted a survey and decided to plant trout in it. That development in essence brought to an end Paul's secret stream.

Other anglers I know have their own secret streams. They share these favorite gems with only a few friends. Andy Leitzinger allowed me to join him on a trek to fish his secret, highly productive water. It was not stocked, and less than 50 miles from downtown Philadelphia. It was ripe with stream-bred browns up to 17 inches long.

Listening to his stories, I watched Andy fish his small, fertile stream. He knew each pool, pocket and boulder. "I caught a 17-inch brown trout there last year," he told me eagerly while we scaled several huge boulders to reach his next honey hole. He told me about the hatches, and on that hot, late-summer afternoon he landed and released 12 beautiful stream-bred trout in two hours. Hiking back to the car, Andy wouldn't walk along the highway that paralleled the stream. He didn't want drivers to see him in his fishing togs, because it might draw too much attention to his secret.

Why keep a stream secret? All of the trout in this water are wild fish. If any are killed, replacing them naturally will take years. Unstocked waters can't stand the killing pressure.

I recently complained, in writing, to the head of the Pennsylvania Fish and Boat Commission because a writer revealed my secret stream in an article. His reply was: You write about streams in your articles; why can't he?

There's a big flaw in that argument: I write about waters with special regulations and planted trout. I don't write about open waters with a good population of wild brown trout and no planted trout and no special regulations. Yes, I eagerly wrote about some of these streams with no regulations and good wild trout populations. But that was a decade ago. I have since seen what increased angling pressure does to these waters and I now look at all of these waters as sacred. I've witnessed good wild trout populations diminish severely. No, I won't write about these waters again.

Secret streams require special care: You have to be careful with whom you share these streams, and make them promise they won't divulge the stream to anyone else. I've taken only three people to my favorite secret stream, all sworn to secrecy. I wanted my friends to experience the same excitement I did the first time I came to this secret stream.

In the fall, if I'm not fly fishing, I'm grouse hunting. I guard my grouse coverts with the same secrecy as I do with my covert streams. I share those with only a few friends and make the not unreasonable demand that the guest must not abuse the discoverer's coverts and honey holes.

One day a friend and I killed four grouse—the state limit—in a morning. I stopped by his house the next morning and his wife told me he and two friends were back "hunting the same area you and he did yesterday." By breaking those hunting and fishing ethics, he lost my trust. I haven't hunted with him since. I do the same with my secret streams—I guard them carefully, and I won't share such stream information with someone I can't trust, either.

When I first fished my secret stream it was a true oddity to see other anglers there. As I fish it now I see more and more anglers discovering it and the fishing quality has definitely gone downhill.

I suppose it's time to move onto the next secret stream. These streams are too precious to have their trout populations decimated by a few anglers who kill everything they catch. Yes, I have more secret streams that I won't write about—and I'll continue not to write about them until they get special no-kill regulations. Only then will I feel that my secret stream will be safe. Until that time these precious waters will remain my secret streams.

Secret streams are found in all areas of the United States. How do you find a secret stream—or at least one that doesn't get the pressure others do? Keep your eyes and ears open. Above all, listen to other anglers. Someone might slip in a sentence describing a fishing trip they recently experienced. Maybe they'll even tell you where it was. Keep your eyes open. Maybe some of those streams that were once polluted have returned. Pollutants include acid mine drainage, chemicals and paper and wood products. Maybe a river polluted 15 years ago is now a vibrant one, teeming with trout.

Austin Morrow lands a trout on a tandem.

I can still remember my childhood river. I played in it, waded in it; but it held no trout because it was polluted with acid mine drainage and coal silt. As youngsters we called it "Black Creek" rather than the Schuylkill River. It deserved the Black Creek appellation. The water was so black you couldn't see bottom in two inches of water. It was a mess. However, recent Pennsylvania anti-pollution laws in have helped this river grow in local prominence as a trout stream. Never in a million years would I have guessed that Black Creek could become a secret stream that holds even brook trout in many locations.

The moral of the story is to protect the resources you have (your secret streams) and keep checking those once-polluted streams. Many of them have recovered from previous episodes of pollution; like the upper end of Clark's Fork near Anaconda, Montana, or the Lackawanna River in Scranton, Pennsylvania. Both now teem with trout.

Chapter 22

The Plastic Man

"ALBERT AND EMERSON OWNED MANY FLY RODS during their lifetimes, but admired none so much as a bamboo rod, which was the rod of their youth."

HARRY MIDDLETON
The Earth is Enough

The Plastic Man

I GAVE UP CASTING THOSE DARNED BAMBOO FLY RODS YEARS AGO. I know that if I really wanted to be a purist, I should cast one of those "tree branches," use a dry fly and fish only when trout rise to a hatch. But I don't.

Many of these bamboo rods are hand-crafted—real works of art. Fishing with a work of art demands special concern for the equipment, I certainly wouldn't want to break a "treasure rod" like that on a stream misstep or an encounter with slick rocks.

I have six wooden fly rods neatly stacked in my fly tying room. I haven't used them or even opened the cases in years. I don't know what kind of shape they're in. I recognized years ago that I'm too heavy-handed for bamboo rods. They have gotten me into trouble in the past. For me, those rods just aren't worth it. I'd probably break one worth $1,000 or more the first time I used it. I was never meant to cast one of those things.

I switched early, and began using a Fenwick fiberglass fly rod in the 1960's. They were great. I had a half dozen fiberglass rods, but when graphite came on the market, I really came to glory. Graphite rods took a lot of abuse—they fit my personality. That's all I use today, because I cast much better with the newfangled "plastic" rods. I don't care what fly rod others cast—I prefer graphite.

Several years ago my fly-fishing friend, Bob Budd, organized a fishing trip in central Pennsylvania for four days in mid-May. We fished a private section of Spruce Creek for two days, then spent another day on Penns Creek, and a half day on Spring Creek. Joining Bob and me were John Gierach, Walt Carpenter, Carl Roszkowski, A.K. Best, and Mike Clark.

John, an eminent fly fishing writer and bamboo rod aficionado, has probably sold more fly fishing books than any other angling guru. Walt and Mike build fly rods—some of the best in the world. Walt takes about 30 orders a years and commands prices well into four figures for his classic bamboo fly rods. Most of Walt's customers feel privileged that Walt will consider them as a client. I'm sure you know who A.K. is—he's also a terrific writer, especially about fly tying. Bob, A.K. and John live in Colorado and came east so John could get some fresh information for more books. Bob Budd, a skilled eye surgeon, is truly one of the finest fly fishers and long distance casters I've ever known. He lives in central Pennsylvania, but his thoughts are often on one of those great steelhead rivers in British Columbia.

When we all got out of our cars at Spruce Creek that first day of the trip, it was fly fisher central. Within a few feet seven of us were assembling our fly rods. I heard a couple of mumbled comments about the plastic man and his fly rod. I assumed they referred to me, since all six of them were busy carefully aligning their $4,000 bamboo fly rod sections.

I alone was fishing a graphite fly rod. And they fished with me, the plastic man, who got his graphite rod free. By the time were headed down to the stream I heard a few other nasty comments about my fishing gear. I overlooked them and figured I'd show them how that piece of plastic caught trout.

We fished private water on Spruce Creek—most of the stream is not open to the public—the first two days, but did poorly. We caught a few fish. But the mid-May Sulfur hatch common on central Pennsylvania waters was halfhearted that year. Things just weren't going well for us.

On the third day, we headed for Penns Creek, to fish below Coburn. Penns gets pounded during mid-May. Anglers know about the great Sulfur and Gray Fox hatches, and realize that they portend the appearance of the Green Drake—the great one—on that stream.

At the 20-car parking area, we couldn't find any parking spaces. Our earlier luck seemed to be holding. Mid-week and no parking…doesn't anyone work anymore? Why were all these people on the stream shortly after noon? Didn't they know the hatch doesn't begin until 8:30 p.m.?

We drove upstream a couple hundred feet and finally found a parking space. Soon some of the other anglers in the parking area heard that John Gierach was there and crowded around him. After a few minutes with these other anglers, all seven of us headed down the abandoned railroad track about a mile and tried to spread out. Although we

Evan Morse lands a trout.

were early, much of the good water had already been taken. Anglers were standing in the good Sulfur hatch sections, reserving them for the evening hatch. Finally, the seven of us spread out and took our places by the bank, semi-reserving sections as long as we stayed by the stream.

Oddly, most of my seven guests just sat by the stream. They decided to wait for the evening hatch. That's the way you fish isn't it? You don't just blatantly go out on the stream and try to drum up a fish, do you?

If you think I'd spend six hours just sitting along a stream waiting for the evening hatch, you're completely wrong. I immediately headed out to a deep, productive-looking riffle and began casting my tandem. I've found the tandem to be a perfect setup when fishing over trout rising to random insects, not part of a hatch. I tied on a Size 12 Patriot dry fly as my indicator and a Size 14 Bead Head Pheasant Tail as my wet fly. The Pheasant Tail looks a lot like the Sulfur nymph and trout had been feeding on that phase of the mayfly for the past couple of nights.

I began casting the duo into a heavy riffle and was rewarded almost immediately. A stream-bred brown hit the wet fly on the second drift. Non-stop action continued throughout that afternoon. While all the others sat back and waited for the hatch, I caught trout—not rising trout, but hungry fish. Some members of our group even took a midday nap. Bob Budd waded into the riffle and he too began catching some big browns that wouldn't wait for the evening hatch. The trout were opportunists—they fed when they saw what they thought was food.

One of the parking lots on Penns Creek during a green drake hatch

About 6 p.m., Bob and I stopped fishing. We'd also wait for the hatch that should appear in a couple hours. John Gierach stopped by and asked when he could expect to see the hatch. I told him it would appear about 8:25 p.m. He laughed and headed back upstream a few hundred yards to a productive-looking riffle. Carl and A.K. also occupied parts of the same riffle.

As the time for the hatch grew near, the crowds increased. Anglers continued to crowd in. What I thought would be a great Sulfur stretch became overpopulated with five other anglers sitting and waiting for the hatch. Where would we all fish? There wasn't enough room for six of us. They didn't care if we had the section first, they just continued to stop there and crowd in on us.

I'd had it. I hate crowd-congested waters, elbow-to-elbow casting. I just hate it. They won. They got me out of there. Just an hour before the expected Sulfur appearance I backed out of the water and hiked upstream to the car. I didn't want any part of this kind of fishing. I would wait at the car if I had to, but I wouldn't put up with this.

At the overloaded parking lot, I looked upstream. A productive-looking riffle had no anglers. Maybe they all thought they had to fish some distance below the parking lot before the fishing got good. Not so. I half jogged to the riffle; because I was afraid someone else would see the vacancy and want the same stretch.

When I arrived, Sulfurs began to appear. I hurried to tie on a Sulfur dry, looked at my watch and saw that the hatch began at 8:28 p.m.—not a bad estimate, remembering what I'd told John to expect.

Straggler Sulfurs filled the riffle and a dozen trout fed on them. It was easy pickings. Just about every one of those trout took that pattern on my plastic fly rod. Maybe if the trout knew I was using graphite they wouldn't have hit my pattern, preferring to be caught on a purist bamboo rod—but the trout didn't seem to care about the differences between bamboo and graphite.

Walt Carpenter quit early, complaining that the stream was too crowded. He gave up on his fishing spot downstream and watched the action unfold in front of me.

I'll remember that evening for a long time: The plastic man found the one empty spot on the stream (right by the parking lot no less), matched the hatch and caught quite a few trout; even when no hatch was active, I caught trout.

We stayed overnight at a lodge near Spruce Creek. John Gierach carried a tiny notebook with him all the time. He jotted notes from time to time and I wondered when and where my comments would appear.

Our final day began with a casting demonstration by John and A. K.. They stood in an open field, testing and casting each other's bamboo fly rods. They even asked me to make a few casts with some of them, and challenged me to try a true "purist's" fly rod. I couldn't say no….and when I began casting the bamboo rod, all of them said, "Look at the plastic man casting that bamboo fly rod." They laughed and laughed. I was perfectly happy to let them laugh. The night before the plastic man showed the bamboo boys that when it comes to Penns Creek Sulfurs, the trout don't care.

Chapter 23
The Power Of The Press

The Power Of The Press

Labor Day weekend, 1984—I was planning for the last fling of summer. My son, Bryan, and I were anticipating three days of fishing. We'd made a trade: I promised to fish for bass one day, then the two of us would fish for trout on the Delaware River and the Beaverkill for two days. I was really looking forward to this, especially to hitting a great Slate Drake hatch on both trout waters.

The weather forecast promised a beautiful weekend, three days of bright blue skies with just a hint of autumn in the air. That very afternoon, we stopped at a truck cap shop in Tunkhannock and bought one. Now we had a place to store our fishing gear. Then we headed for Towanda, Pennsylvania and the upper Susquehanna River.

Bryan is a great bass fisherman. He even travels to an occasional bass tournament. September is a hot month for smallmouth bass on the river. That time of year smallmouths gorge themselves, preparing for winter. We agreed to fish the river at the north end of Towanda Friday evening, then head towards the Beaverkill. We parked our truck and walked about a half mile to a productive riffle. In two hours of fishing, the riffle gave up plenty of smallmouths, caught on my Black Wooly Bugger. Bryan caught a dozen bass on a combination of spinners and plugs, and we had a great evening of fishing.

We returned to the truck early, to get an early start for New York, the Delaware and the Beaverkill. Approaching the truck, I saw the door on the cap open and I accused Bryan of forgetting to close it. He said he had closed it. The closer we got, the more apprehensive I became. Why was the door open?

I soon saw why the door was open. Nothing—and I mean nothing—but our two small suitcases remained. The thief had even opened the suitcases and scattered the contents about the bed of the truck. Someone had stolen our gear, and even searched through our suitcases looking for valuables. Five fly rods, five reels—gone. The culprit took my compartmented fly box and Bryan's fly box. We'd worn our boots and vests or they would have vanished, too. In full daylight, in a fairly open place, someone had stolen all our fly-fishing gear.

What to do? We immediately went to the Towanda Police station in midtown.

The officers asked where the truck was parked; they told us they had experienced a rash of break-ins nearby. I asked why a warning hadn't been posted, but got no answer. I asked when we might get our gear back, and the answer was non-committal. They indicated that five thefts in that area remained unsolved. They also said they couldn't spend much time on the incident; there were more important items to look into. We'd lost about $3,000 in fly-fishing gear and the police were too busy to investigate?

I swore the culprits wouldn't get away with it. The police asked what I planned to do and I said they'd see in a few days.

Bryan and I returned home, our trip cancelled for lack of gear and a loss of appetite for fishing for a while. The theft had left a bad taste in our mouths.

After I returned home, I composed an open letter to the citizens of the Towanda area. In the letter, I gave a complete, detailed list of every item taken—every brand name on every fly rod and reel—and indicated that most of the stolen items were my 16-year-old son's. I explained how he'd earned the money to buy the gear cutting neighbors' lawns. I asked that anyone who knew anything about the incident contact the Towanda police, and I sent the letter to the *Towanda Review*, the town's daily newspaper.

The newspaper printed my letter on the Saturday morning front page. Within an hour of the newspaper hitting the streets, I got a call from a lady in Towanda. She said her son was given one of the reels I'd listed, and she had called the police and gave them the name of the thief. She wouldn't give me her name. She wanted to keep out of it as much as possible.

The next morning the police, armed with a warrant, raided the thief's home, discovering every item that had been taken from us and more. The thief had many other fishing items he'd stolen from cars and trucks in the lot, plus dozens of other items he had taken from other fishermen in that same general vicinity. The police called after the raid and told me they had recovered all my gear. Not once did they thank me for what I had done, but they did say they needed the confiscated goods for a couple weeks as evidence. They also let me know that the 22-year-old criminal wasn't home when they searched his house. The police said he was camping on an island on the river. The next morning they arrested him on the island.

When the police brought the young criminal to the courthouse for his arraignment, he escaped—just walked out on the police. They recaptured him about six months later when he came back to Towanda to wait in line for an unemployment check. The police asked if I'd testify against the young crook. I agreed. He ended up with a two-year prison sentence.

Although our Delaware River and Beaverkill trip had to wait a year, we did hit a spectacular hatch of Slate Drakes and some hungry Delaware rainbows.

The moral of this story? First and foremost, don't depend on flimsy tailgate doors to protect your gear. Second, keep all your gear out of sight. Hide it in the front of the truck behind the seat. Third, try to park in a well-lighted public area. Finally, if authorities are too busy to do anything with your case, don't hesitate to take it into your own hands. They have thousands of cases to investigate—yours is only one of them. Try to circulate, preferably through the media, a list of the stolen items. Be specific and do it as soon as possible after the theft.

I was certainly robbed—the burglar took much of my better fly-fishing gear. I could have sat back and waited, while probably nothing would have happened to resolve the case—it simply wasn't an important enough incident. Without the help of the local newspaper, that crime probably would never have been solved. With the help of the local paper, the crime was solved within an hour…a good demonstration of the power of the press.

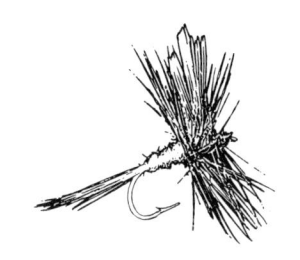

Bryan Meck fishing during a Green Caddis hatch.

BIBLIOGRAPHY

• Brooks, Charles E, 1976, *Nymph Fishing for Larger Trout*,
New York, The Lyons Press.

• Caucci, Al & Nastasi, Bob, 1986, *Hatches II*,
New York, Lyons & Buford.

• Gordon, Theodore, 1966, *American Trout Fishing*,
New York, Alfred A. Knopf.

• Leiser, Eric & Boyle, Robert H. 1982, *Stoneflies for the Angler*,
Harrisburg, PA, Stackpole Books.

• Lyons, Nick, *The Quotable Fisherman*,
New York, The Lyons Press.

• Marinaro, Vincent C., 1976, *In the Ring of the Rise*,
Guilford, CT, The Globe Pequot Press.

• Meck, Charles R., 1995, *Patterns Hatches, Tactics and Trout*,
Williamsport, PA, Vivid Publishing.

• Middleton, Harry, 1996, *The Earth is Enough*
Boulder, CO, Pruett.

• Schwiebert, Ernest G., Jr., 1955, *Matching the Hatch*
South Hackensack, NJ, Stoeger Publishing.

INDEX

—A—
A Modern Dry Fly Code 37
Abrams Creek 171
Adams 158, 193
Adams, Ed 172
Alder, Montana 88, 195
Allenberry Resort 204
Anaconda, Montana 229
Arch Spring
Bed & Breakfast 177
Arizona 169
Arizona Trout Streams And Their Hatches 109
Armstrong, Jerry 195
Astra-Zeneca 98
Au Sable River 67

—B—
Baird, Rev. Larry 91
Bald Eagle Creek 87
Bassett, Darryl 203
Bay, Mike 185
Baylor, Don 18
Bead Head Glow Bug 172
Bead Head Pheasant Tail 205
Bead Head Tan Caddis 91
Bear Creek 213
Beaver Creek 203
Beaverkill 128, 243
Beck, Barry 37
Beck, Cathy 37
Becoming a Fly Fisher 119
Bedford 58
Bellefonte 18
Bellwood, Penna. 121
Best, A. K. 235
Best, Raymond 78
bicolor Trico spinner 100
Bighorn River 183
Biology of Mayflies 159
Bitterroot River 68
Black Caddis 206
"Black Creek" 229
Black Stonefly 29
Black Wooly Bugger 243
Blackburn, David 184
Blue Quill 58
Blue Ribbon Anglers 70
Blue-winged Olives 98
Bob's Creek 58
Boiling Springs 118

Boltz Knitting Mills 213
Borger, Gary 203
Bower, Wes 88
Bowman Creek 39
Bradford,
Virgil 6, 110, 171, 172
Broomfield, Patrick 78
Brown Drake 9
Budd, Bob 6, 197
Buffalo 91
Busch, Jack 218
Bush (1st)
Administration 57

—C—
Cache la Poudre River 127
Caenis 147
Caldwell Creek 218
Camera, Phil 226
Carlisle, Penna. 174
Carpenter, Walt 235
Carper, John 58
Casper, Wyoming 205
Catskills 128
Cedar Run 87, 161
Chambersburg 37
Charlie Brooks 69
Cheney, Dick 10, 57
Cheney Pool 61
Christchurch 25
Cilletti, Fred 57
Clarion River 169
Clark, Mike 235
Clark's Fork 229
Coburn 236
Coffin Flies 47
Coles, Ralph 78
Colorado River 127
Continuing Education 138
Conyngham, Guthrie 15
Conyngham, Jack 15
Cooper, Jack & Lorraine 78
Cottonwood, Ariz. 100, 159
Countryman Press 138
Coyne, Todd 98
Craig, Montana 185
Crawford, Tom 139
Cutbows 172
Czonka, Larry 176

—D—
Dallas, Penna. 157
Davis, Mark 48, 128, 214
Dead Horse State Park 100
Delle Donne,
Nick and Beverly 140
Deschutes River 184, 186
Desert Storm 62
Dette, Mary 226
Dillon, Montana 177
Dingle Burn 26
DuBois, Penna. 139

—E—
Early Brown Stonefly 29
Eglinton Rivers 27
Eighteen Mile Creek 91
Elam, Pat 185
Elevenmile Reservoir 226
Elk Creek 158
Engerbrettson,
Dave 175, 205
Ephemera guttulata 80
Epstein, Charlie 15
Erie, Penna. 97
Eshenower, Dave 226
ESPN/Suzuki Outdoors 176
Espy's farm 128
Evening Rise Fly Shop 140

—F—
Falling Springs Creek 37
Falls Creek, Penna. 139
Federation of
Fly Fishers 131
Fishing Small Streams With a Fly Rod 170
Fishing Yellowstone Waters 69
Flick, Art 159
Fly Fisherman
(magazine) 119
Flyfisher's Paradise 140
Fornwalt, Don 48
Fort Bragg, N. Carolina 160
Fort Collins, Colorado 170
Fox, Charlie 38

—G—
Gardiner, Montana 70
Gehman, Tony 226
Gierach, John 235

Glow Bug 88
Goldman, Andrew 57
Goose Bay 77
Grand Canyon 98
Granite Reef 108
Grannom 147
Gray Fox 147, 236
Great Rivers—
Great Hatches 107, 183
Green Caddis 225
Green Drake 9
Green River 183
Green Weenie 204
Greene, Tom 216
Guptill, Howard 78

—H—
Hagen, John 15
Hancock,
 New York 217, 226
Harvey, George 37
Harvey's Lake 87
Hawthorne, Jim 119
Heltzel, Jim 162
Hendrickson 10
Henry, Dick 193
Henry's Fork 70, 147
Hexagenia rigida 80
Hilligas, Donna 49
Hitterman, Gary 6
Hoagland Branch 160
Holiday Inn 139
Hoover,
 Greg 129, 175, 183
Howe, Bill 110
Hurricane Agnes 128, 130

—I—
Idaho 169
Isaak's Ranch 175

—J—
Johnson, Clyde 138, 193
Josephson, Craig
 6, 60, 100, 119, 171

—K—
Kapolka, Jay 186
Kohl's Ranch 171
Kootenai 184
Krouse, Andrew 119

—L—
Labrador 77
Lackawanna
 River 219, 229
Lake Te Anau 27

Lancaster, Penna. 140
Lee's Ferry 127
Leitzinger, Andy 150
LeTort Spring Creek 38
Libby, Montana 184
Light Cahill 16
Light Cahills 128
Light, Julie 91
Little Blue-winged
 Olives 107, 28
Little Juniata River 119
Little Juniata River
 Association 131
Love's Canoe Rental 169
Lumsden, New Zealand 27

—M—
Madison River 120
Manfredo, Mike 25, 170
March Brown 16, 87
Marinaro, Vince 37, 194
Matauira River 28
Matching The Hatch 159
Matolyak, Bruce 6
Mayflies of Michigan 159
McDonald,
 Jake & Donna 89, 195
McDonald, Steve 6, 77
McFarland, Mike 121
McFarland Rod
 Company 121
McKenzie boats 184
McKenzie River 186
McMullen, Dave 57
McMullen, Joe 215
Meck Family
 Bryan (son)
  6, 58, 88, 98, 218
 Harold 6
 Jerry 6, 184
 Shirley 6, 26, 50, 87
 Ted 6
*Meeting and Fishing the
 Hatches* 67, 70, 137
Melby, Eric 91
Mesa, Arizona 108
Metolius River 186
Michaels, Frank 17
*Mid-Atlantic Fly Fishing
 Guide* 175
Mills, Dick 16, 38
Mingerell, Bill 91
Minipi River 80
Minshall, Ned 48
Missoula, Montana 67
Missouri River 183

Misuira, Jim 219
Mogollon Rim 109
Monasterio, Manuel 172
Mont Alto Campus 138
Montella, Richie 185
Morrow, Austin 177
Morrow, David 177
Mowry, Russ 6
Mt. Cook, New Zeal. 27
Muddler Minnow 16, 176

—N—
Needham 159
Needhami duns 163
New Mexico 169
New Zealand 25
Nicholas, Nick 70
Nofer, Frank 6
North Mountain Club 128
North Platte River 119
Novotny, Al 205
Nowaczek, Rick 60
*Nymph Fishing for
 Larger Trout* 69
Nymphs 129

—O—
Oak Creek 107
Oil Creek 97
O'Keefe, Shawn 57
Olive Bead Head Caddis 90
Olive Sulfur 163
Omarama 25
Oregon 169
Oreti River 28
Orvis 16

—P—
Pale Morning Dun 62
Paradise, Penna. 140
Patriot (fly) 88, 196
Payson, Arizona 171
Penn State
 University 15, 17
Penns
 Creek 48, 129, 147, 236
*Pennsylvania
 Angler & Boater* 19
Pennsylvania
 Dutch Country 140
Pennsylvania Fish &
 Boat Commission 216
Pennsylvania Outdoor
 Writers Association 87
*Pennsylvania Trout and
 Salmon Guide* 140

250

Pennsylvania Trout Streams 140
Pennsylvania Trout Streams And Their Hatches 57
Peppers, Jake 171
Perhach, John 16
Phantom Canyon 170
Pheasant Tail 205, 237
Philadelphia, Penna. 150
Phoenix, Arizona 97, 109
Pine Creek 159
Pine Creek Watershed Association 163
Pittsburgh, Penna. 203
Poindexter's Slough 178
Pottsville, Penna. 213
PBS 205

—Q—
Queenstown, New Zeal. 27
Quigley, Ed 77
Quill Gordon 16, 28

—R—
Randolph, John 119, 157
Ray Thomas Award for Conservation 48
Reading, Penna. 226
Red Bank Creek 139
Red Quill 16
Red River 172
Redline, Harry 225
Rictor, Ken 89
Ridgway 169
Ring of the Rise 37
Rocky Mountains 67
Rodriguez, Don 170
Roszkowski, Carl 235
Rotz, Lynn 89
Royal Coachman 16, 158
Ruby River 89, 195

—S—
Saguaro Lake 108
Sajna, Mike 140
Salmon Flies 70
Salt River 98, 107
San Juan River 183, 184
Santa Fe, New Mexico 172
Schuylkill River 229
Schweibert, Jr., Ernest 159
Scranton, Penna. 97, 229
Seattle, Washington 205
Sedona, Arizona 107
Serviente, Barry 174
Sesow, Pete 100

Sharon, Penna. 97
Sheridan, Montana 120
Show Low, Arizona 109
Shuman, Craig 205
Silver Creek 109, 183
Simple Salmon 70
Sinking Creek 177
Six Springs 57
Slate Drake 138, 193
Slate Run 161
Smallmouth bass 118
Smoky Mountains 171
Snow, Chad 78
Snowden, Rollie 15
South Island, New Zeal. 29
South Platte River 226
Spring Creek 18
Spruce Creek 57, 128
Spruce Creek Tavern 58
Spruce Creek trout hatchery 215
Stackpole Books 183
Stan Cooper 15
State College 25, 140
State College Hotel 61
Stinky and Pugh 195
Streamside Guide 159
Stroudsburg, Penna. 18
Sulfur 18
Sunbury, Penna. 175
Susquehanna River 118
Syracuse, New York 100

—T—
Tan caddis 90
Taos 172
Taylor, Carl 138
Taylor, Tom 6, 157, 161
"The Early Grays" 109
"The Encampment" 203
Nature Conservancy 170
The Travel Channel 205
The Trout and the Stream 69
Titusville, Penna. 97
Tonto Creek 127, 171
Towanda, Penna. 243
Towanda Review 244
Townsend, Tennessee 171
Trico 10, 98
Troth, Al 177
Trout Flies 130
Tulpehocken Creek 226
Tulpehocken Creek Outfitters 226
Tunkhannock, Penna. 138
Turner, Ted 195

—U—
Ultimate Flyfishers.com 217
Uniontown, Penna. 203
Upper Canyon Outfitters 88
Upper Canyon Ranch 195

—V—
Valley of the Sun 97
Verde River 98, 101
Victor, Montana 68

—W—
Waikaia River 28
Washington (state of) 169
Washington State University 205
Weamer, Paul 6, 217
Wellsboro, Penna. 87
West Yellowstone 69
Wetzel, Charles 130, 175
White Fly 117
Wilkes-Barre, Penna. 15
Willamette River 186
Williams, Brian 110
Williams, Lloyd 6, 157, 161
Williamson River 184, 186
Willowemoc River 128
Winchester Press 67
Wolfe, Rick 176
Woodring, Lois and Lori 59
Wooly Bugger 16
Worsley River 27
WPSX-TV 176

—Y—
Yakima River 205
Yellow Breeches Creek 38, 118
Yellow Breeches Anglers Club 204
Yellow Drakes 128
Yellow Sally 213
Yellowstone National Park 69

—Z—
Zebra Midge 98